Splintered
HEART

CRISTY L. PATERNO

ISBN 978-1-7358908-2-1 (paperback)
ISBN 978-1-7358908-3-8 (eBook)

Chapter One

———◆———

The train danced slowly down the rail, like an old overweight woman, puffing smoke into the Oklahoma night sky. The train had different compartments, depending on the affluence of the passengers. There was a different caliber of passengers; from the middle class to the low class. In one of the budget-friendly compartments, a black-haired woman sat in one of the cabins, which she shared with three other passengers.

With lean long fingers, she gripped on to her satchel, as though her life depended on it. Perhaps her life did depend on it, because the meager sum in the satchel, was her whole life savings. Sandy as she was called, had cleaned up her life in Tulsa, Oklahoma, and put it in a box; it was time to search for greener pastures. She heard that New York was a city of possibilities and miracles, and so she had set her sights on that city. The tune of Alicia Keys' song 'Empire State of Mind,' filtered into her mind and she began to hum the tune.

"New York...where dreams are made of...there is nothing you can't doooh..." she mumbled, attracting the stare of the middle-aged woman sitting by her side.

The middle-aged woman, with a face too tight from too many Botox treatments, sized Sandy up. How she wished she had Sandy's caramel brown skin and beautiful full lips.

"I will need to get the doctor to inject my lips if I want those full lips," the woman thought grudgingly. Her eyes roamed over Sandy's small waist and almost flat midsection; she could almost swear that

1

Sandy got her well-kept body weight from going under the knife, but one look at Sandy's plain clothes, told her the young woman could not afford it.

"Are you going to New York for the first time?" the woman asked, flashing a cheery smile.

"Yes, it is my first time," Sandy replied with a reluctant smile of her own. She had seen the woman's eyes all over her body and was wondering if she was a lesbian.

"First-timers are always expectant, but really, we make our destinies, not the city," the woman gave Sandy a piece of unsolicited advice.

Sandy did not care about this woman's advice, as she was sure her life would turn around if she moved to New York. Nevertheless, she would remember this woman's advice and it would guide her actions. For now, Sandy reclined into the upholstery and closed her eyes. She did not doze off, but saw her life play before her eyes, like in a movie. Her life had not gone on as she planned, in fact, everything that could go wrong did. She just got out of a relationship in which she invested three years of her life. The man whom she thought loved her as much as she did, only realized after three years that they were not compatible. She had kept hoping that he would miss her and see how much she had become a part of his life. But she got an awakening when she found out on social media, that he was getting married. She realized then what had happened.

When she was a teenager, she had many dreams about how her life would go. She would finish college, get a job in one of the big companies in Oklahoma, buy a sleek car and a penthouse, have a great body that would land her a rich, handsome man for marriage at age twenty-four. She would make her parents proud. But here she was, at twenty-eight, unmarried, broke and not knowing what shape her life would take. Even though she had graduated from college with a BS degree, there was no car and no high paying job. She had to take the bus every day, from her dingy apartment to the industrial district, where she worked as a sales manager in a boutique. She had not made her parents proud as she had planned but instead had become the butt of jokes at every family dinner.

"We should probably take Sandy to be exorcised because I think she is cursed," her grandmother had said at one Thanksgiving dinner. "Look at Thelma, the Watson's daughter. She works in Washington now and last I heard, she has snagged herself a rich beau, whose father is a senator."

That had been the beginning of a long discussion about her hard luck.

It was not as if she was not approached by men. She had been through a lot of relationships, which always ended in heartbreaks. It was either the men were just looking out for fun, or they were not ready for marriage and so never brought up the subject of marriage, no matter how many years they spent together.

When Sandy could not take it anymore, she decided to leave Oklahoma for New York. She did not have any plans, she only knew she would survive somehow. If only she knew what awaited her.

After three days on the road, the train got to the Grand Central terminal. Sandy took her luggage and left, walking into the rising sun. She felt lost, but at the same time, she felt like she made the best decision of her entire life.

"Taxi!" she called out, waving helplessly as the cabs sped away. Then she turned and saw a young woman flag down a cab. She looked so confident as she posed with legs apart, with her big thumb in front of her. Sandy wondered if she would ever be like this woman, after years living in New York; confident, beautiful, and sexy.

She was still pondering on this when a cab stopped in front of her. "Where are you going?" the Black cab driver asked. He had a familiar accent and Sandy did not search her brain for long before she associated it with the Nigerian immigrant her neighbor back in Tulsa dated.

"Uhm...I don't know," Sandy stuttered.

"What?" the cab driver looked at her as if she was mad, but when he saw her luggage, he realized she was new. "Hop in!"

As the cab sped away with Sandy in it, the driver told her where she could get a hotel to stay in. As he spoke, he sized her up, as if he was trying to ascertain if she could afford a hotel room. Her well-worn denim trousers and chiffon blouse did not convince him of this fact, because he told her where she could get a cheap motel.

"I need an apartment," Sandy said, and as a second thought, she said, "a cheap one."

"Are you here for good?" the driver asked, giving her a side glance.

"Am I?" Sandy pondered as she watched the tall buildings of the city, fly past. Her eyes shimmered with wonder and hope.

"I am here for good." Sandy had already fallen in love with the city and decided she would not bail on her new city, no matter what she faced here.

"If so, I know a good agent that can get you an apartment...that fits your budget," the driver replied and searched in his glove box. He brought out a card and slipped it into her hand.

"Thank you, you have been more than helpful." As Sandy said this, she believed that the driver was sent to her as a sign that her stay in New York would be good, or so she thought.

Sandy was still looking out the window at the beautiful city when the cab stopped in a light 'drive and stop' congestion. Her eyes went to the car beside theirs and fell on a handsome, brown-haired, bloke. He was talking on the phone and had a serious look on his face, which made him all cuter. His car showed he was rich, and from his mannerism, she could tell he was born into wealth.

"Not your league," Sandy thought. Just before coming to New York, she had read a Red Pill post about sex market value, where they told a woman or man, how desirable they could be to a prospective mate. Sandy knew that a rich, handsome man like this stranger, would go for the plastic girls, with shiny blonde hair, creamy skin, a walk-in closet, and of course a trust fund. He could not roll with a plain Jane like her.

As if her thoughts had gotten to the stranger, he turned and stared right at her. She averted her eyes immediately and caught the cab driver chuckling.

"That was awkward," Sandy quipped and blew her hair out of her face.

She pulled down the sun visor and stared at her face in the mirror attached to it. She had gotten high cheekbones from her mother, and a perfect set of white teeth. Everyone said she had a beautiful smile and she did not doubt them. Her lips were full and dimpled, with brown eyes that had a light in them. Some people would call her beautiful, except they loved the airbrushed pictures of celebrities and models.

Her first week in New York, Sandy spent almost all her savings on renting an apartment. The apartment was not much different from the one she had in Tulsa. It was small, and could only allow a bed, but it also had a kitchen and toilet. She did not have anything saved for her luggage and so, she did not mind the space. Her only problem with the apartment was the fact that it faced a busy road and so the traffic sounds were unbearable. The first week, she could hardly sleep through the night, and sometimes she found herself crying. Her life was bad, and she needed a break.

After looking for job vacancies in every establishment she was allowed into, Sandy slipped into a quaint coffee shop. The shop looked like her mother's homey kitchen back in Tulsa, with the table decorated with hand-knitted mats. She ordered coffee and croissants. Looking around the coffee shop, she could not help but notice that most of the women in the shop spotted rings on their fourth fingers. One of the women even had a giant diamond rock on her fourth finger. Sandy found herself envying them and wishing that her luck was that bright. Coming to New York, she thought it would be bright and sunny in her life, but no, she was not getting any headway with her plans and she was so lonely.

"Hey!" the voice broke into her thoughts.

When Sandy looked up, she saw a sassy looking woman, with flowing silky red hair. She looked straight out of a Vogue magazine, with her emerald-colored eyes and plump, pout lips. The stranger had a big smile on her face, which flaunted her perfect set of teeth.

"Hi...hi" Sandy stuttered.

"You have been looking into space and you have 'newbie,' written all over you. This is New York, no one gets lonely here," the woman said. "I am Hailey and I am here with my friends. Would you like to join us?"

"Am I that obvious?" Sandy looked towards where she was pointing and saw two women chatting, with hot, drippy burgers in front of them. They waved at her when she caught their eyes, and she smiled at them.

"That you are new in the city? Yes! Now come on," Hailey replied.

At the table, the two women introduced themselves as Bridget and Spencer. They were as beautiful and sassy as Hailey and they did not look broke like her. The shift she chose for the day began to feel inadequate compared to these women's designer clothes. They told her to taste the cupcakes made at the coffee shop and when she tried to refuse because she did not want to go beyond her budget, they told her it was their treat and she could not refuse. It was the beginning of a beautiful friendship that would see her through all her hardest times.

One day Sandy met with yet another disappointment in finding a job, so she retired to her small apartment. She whiled away the evening counting the few dollar notes left from her life savings, which she brought to New York.

"Something has got to give soon, or I am going to starve," Sandy thought, running her hands through her hair, which was dry because she had nothing to spare for hair products.

Just then her phone rang with Hailey's call. She picked it up and immediately Hailey could tell she was not happy.

"What's wrong?" Hailey asked.

"I still have not found a job and I am tired of visiting you three just because I want to eat," Sandy replied.

"I think we should go out tonight. It is the weekend, we can worry about finding a job for you on Monday," Hailey said.

"Hailey, I am not in the mood." Sandy looked at the fold-able wardrobe which held clothes she couldn't wear for a night out in New York.

"When we are done, you would be in the mood," Hailey replied.

"We what?" Sandy tried to ask, but Hailey had hung up already.

In thirty minutes the whole gang was at Sandy's apartment. They had brought a sequined dress for her and a makeup kit.

"Get into the shower and make sure you wash your hair," Amy said and flung a bottle of hair conditioner at her.

After her shower, the girls put her in front of a mirror and went to work on her. They worked on her hair until it was silky soft and shined with a dark glow and then it cascaded in soft curls down her back. They also did a makeover on her face, accentuating her cheekbone. Her lackluster eyes glimmered under the smoky eye makeup and her lips had been contoured to look plump. When they were done, Sandy dressed up in the sequined dress and a pair of strapped high heel sandals.

"Oh my God!" she exclaimed when she opened her eyes to her image in the mirror. It looked like a beautiful stranger was staring back at her.

"We have to get going now or we are going to lose our VIP spot," Hailey said looking at her watch.

"They have gone through so much trouble to cheer me up. I might as well relax and have some fun," Sandy thought, as she threw her inhibitions off the window. This night would be the night of her life.

They had hired a driver for the night and he drove them to the Lavo nightclub. Hailey chose this club because of the restaurant on the top floor; she wanted them to have dinner before they went down to the club. They had dinner at the restaurant as Hailey planned and then as the night has worn on, they went down to the bustling club. Sandy had to hold herself, so she did not embarrass herself; she had never been in a place like this before.

As the girls walked into the club, all eyes were on them, especially Sandy. She was looking gorgeous, more than she ever thought possible. They have serviced drinks on rocks, as the music boomed from the speakers. People were already filling the dance floor. Sandy did not drink alcohol and despite the pressure from her friends to drink tonight, she stuck to her cherry drink. Unknown to her, the girls were tired of her stiffness and wanted her to have some fun. So, they had slipped a party drug in her drink. Slowly, Sandy moved her body to the beat, but soon she went to the center of the dance floor and began to dance, *twerking* to the beat, with moves no one thought possible of Sandy. All eyes were on her, including his eyes. He had noticed she had ordered a cherry drink and it had gotten him intrigued because it was hard to find a woman in New York who did not drink.

"I think my bladder is going to give out," Sandy said and staggered towards the restroom, but she never got there.

Sandy could barely stand straight as she staggered to the restroom. "How does cherry make you feel drunk?" she thought, wondering why she was so inebriated. Then she slammed into hard rock and felt herself falling fast. She did not know what it was, but she felt consciousness slipping out of her. However, before the darkness enveloped her, she caught the face of the stranger, the same one she had seen in traffic, on her first day in New York.

"What did you give her? She was having a cherry drink!" she heard the voice. It was demanding, probably angry, but it had a rich note that made her insides tingle.

"We just wanted her to have fun." It was Hailey's voice and she sounded worried.

Sandy tried to stay awake, as she felt lifted off the ground, but her eyes dropped in drowsiness.

Chapter Two

Sandy woke with a start; she looked at the plush bedroom and knew immediately she was not in her apartment. It did not look like any of the bedrooms of her friends, so she got out of bed. It was only then she realized she was wearing an over-sized shirt.

"Oh my God, did I get a one-night stand?" Where am I?" Sandy asked, looking around the room, where she had woken up.

"You are safe," a voice said. It was the same voice she heard before she went unconscious.

She turned and stared into the brown eyes of the most handsome guy she ever met. She saw his muscled chest and knew it was the hard rock she had slammed into. He was tall, with a well-toned body and a face that looked like he had caused many women sleepless nights. He looked like the Greek gods that had decorated her college dorm, with a chiseled face and mischievous, daring eyes. His pale lips sported a smirk like he was in on a private joke.

"Hi, I am Damian." He waved a hand in front of her face to bring her back to focus. "What do you remember?" He was curt, but the curtness did not reach his eyes, because they were tender.

Sandy felt as if she could drown in the brown depths of his eyes.

When he saw she was not saying anything, he ran his hands through his dark brown hair. As he did this, the musky smell of his cologne wafted into her nostrils. It was a heady smell and made her legs go weak. She stumbled, but he grabbed her before she could reach the ground, pulling her close. This proximity only made her the more intoxicated, as she was hit with the smell of hay and horses.

Mixed with his cologne, it was a masculine smell that made Sandy begin to pant.

"Your friends put a party drug in your drink last night and I think we should get you checked into a hospital," he said, looking at her with concern.

"What!" Sandy pushed herself off his arms. She was annoyed by the fact that her friends had taken the fun too far. "I only remember fainting." She stopped before she would spill the fact that she also remembered his face and voice.

"I don't think it is necessary to go to the hospital. I will be fine with coffee," Sandy said further.

"While you were sleeping, I took the liberty to get your clothes. They are in the walk-in closet. Shower and meet me downstairs," Damian said and left the bedroom.

"Wow," Sandy thought. Looking around the house, she realized that Damian was affluent. He was in a class she had never been in. She was so poor, and he was so rich.

What she did not know, is that Damian is the heir of a powerful New York family, Remington. They had made money in just about any industry but were popularly known for their energy company and horses. They had the biggest horse farm in Hampton and millions of dollars in real estate. The house where he brought Sandy was just one of the many houses the family had scattered all over New York. He had been on the cover of several entertainment magazines, as one of the trust fund heirs, who would never be broke in their lives. Damian had never worked in his life; he was on the board of the Rem Energy company, but everything he had was tied to the family.

Sandy went to the spotless, state-of-the-art bathroom, and had her bath. Afterward, she went to the walk-in closet and found a navy-blue cashmere top and a pair of white pant trousers hanging on a chaise. The closet was stocked with different brands of shoes, clothes, watches, perfumes, and so on.

"Why did he bring me here?" Sandy pondered as she dressed up.

When she was done, she looked at herself in the mirror and was happy with what she saw. Her hair still looked silky after Hailey's work on it and the color of the cashmere top complimented her eyes.

She heard the door open and rushed out of the closet.

Damian drove them in his sleek BMW to Sant Ambroeus, an upscale coffee shop that also served Italian cuisine. Sandy had the most expensive mocha latte she ever tasted. While they ate the lasagna Damian had ordered, he watched her intensely. There was a worried look in her eyes and he did not know why.

"You look worried," Damian broke the silence.

"I am all right." Sandy forced a smile on her face, but Damian could see through her.

"Something is bothering you. Do you think I took advantage of you? I am a gentleman and as the heir of the Remington family, I cannot afford to cause scandal to my family," Damian replied.

"Remington, who are they?" Sandy asked.

"You don't know my family. Oh, how sweet" Damian ran his fingers through his hair in exasperation, but it made Sandy want to touch them and feel their silkiness.

"I am new in the city, so forgive my ignorance."

"My family is one of the billionaire families in New York. We own Rem Energy and the largest horse farm in the Hampton, besides other business endeavors"

He sounded smug as he talked, but Sandy did not mind. She was too struck by him to care about any bad traits.

They talked all through the morning until the sun was way up in the sky. It was as if they had known each other for a long time. Damian was impressed that she knew a little about everything; it was the trait he often looked for in his women.

He had dated different girls, but they were mostly from rich families. They were all trust fund heirs like him and never had to work or learn anything for that matter. There was only one woman who had been from a rich family like him yet made an impression on him.

"Nicole..." Damian shrugged the memory away.

He had loved Nicole, but they had drifted apart, despite the effort by both families to keep them together and even get them married. Their marriage would have consolidated the two families and their businesses and made them stronger.

Perhaps he could have a fling with Sandy, just so he would know what it felt like to date a woman who had no inheritance or a respected family name. He would not know, that his action would start a series of events that would change the course of both their lives.

"What do you do?" Damian asked.

"I am..." Sandy started to lie because she did not want to sound like a broke failure without a job, but she thought better of it. "I have not found a job yet."

"Oh, I can help you with that. I am sure there is somewhere you can fit in any of our companies," Damian replied.

"You would do that. But you hardly know me," Sandy retorted, wondering why he was being overly nice.

"I want to know you. You intrigue me in a sort of way." He stared into her eyes as if he was trying to decode her. "I know a nice Karaoke bar we can go this evening, what do you say?"

"Yes," Sandy replied. There was no doubt she already liked him.

When Sandy stepped into her apartment, it felt like she had been thrown from heaven to hell. She smiled however when she remembered the man she had met through a chance encounter and she could not wait to meet him again.

"I guess I should thank Hailey and the others...if it weren't for the drug, I probably would not have stumbled into Damian," Sandy soliloquized.

"You are crazy, Sandy. Don't act thirsty," she berated herself as she went about tidying her apartment.

When her phone rang, her heart skipped a beat because she thought it was Damian calling. But when she picked up the phone, she saw it was Spencer, the blonde in their girl gang.

"Hi Spence, how are you?"

"I should be asking you," Spencer said. "I was against leaving you with that man, but Hailey said she felt good about him. He is eye candy though."

"He sure is!" Sandy exclaimed and giggled.

"You are giggling! Oh my God, did you do the deed?"

"What deed are you talking about? Damian is a responsible man."

"And a hot catch...do you know who he is? He is the most eligible bachelor in New York City," Spencer said.

"He sure is." Sandy heard Amy say.

"Is this a conference call?" Sandy looked at her phone and saw that the whole gang was on a conference call.

"It sure is...didn't you know? You need to sleep that drug off."

"I need to sleep, but most importantly, I need to prepare for my date," Sandy retorted.

"Oh my! You have caught yourself a rich man," Hailey said, and the rest joined in cheering her.

She wanted to tell them that not only was Damian interested in her, he also wanted to get her a job. She did not want to seem like she was a gold digger, because even if Damian was not the rich man he was, she would still date him.

"He is so cool...almost perfect!" Sandy said aloud and realized too late that she had spoken out loud.

"Something serious happened last night. Our girl is head over heels," Spencer said.

"Tell us all the sexy, little details!" Amy quipped.

"There is nothing to tell! We just talked a lot this morning. I was knocked out all through the night. Come on!" Sandy replied.

They agreed to come over, so they could go shop for an outfit for the date, but before they could come, Sandy got herself a surprise.

She had just gotten off the call with her girlfriends when there came a knock on her door. She was sure her friends had not suddenly developed wings and flown to her apartment, neither was she expecting a visitor.

"Perhaps it is my neighbor again," Sandy said in a barely audible tone as she reluctantly went to the door. The apartment facing hers was occupied by a scrawny young man, with a protuberant Adam apple, who was always knocking on her door and asking for things.

Flinging the door wide open, she came face to face with Damian. He had a large bouquet of yellow tulips and a shopping bag in hand. "I couldn't wait until the evening before I saw you again. Besides I wanted to bring this," he said as an explanation.

"Oh, come in." Sandy managed an uncomfortable smile and looked back at her shoebox apartment.

"Don't worry, I don't plan on staying. Wear the dress tonight," Damian said and passed the shopping bag and the bouquet to her.

"How did you know my address and the fact that I love tulips?" Sandy asked.

"I told you I wanted to know you and so I went digging." Damian flashed her a wry smile.

Sandy felt giddy with excitement at the fact that Damian was interested in her. She remembered the Red Pill articles she had read and decided that they were wrong. A man that was out of her league could find her interesting.

"It is probably just for the sex," a voice in her mind said, but she pushed it away. If it were only for sex, he would have taken advantage of her drugged state.

"You could charge him for rape and he does have a family name to protect. Talking about protecting his family name, you are not exactly the stellar girlfriend material for a man like him. It would be scandalous," the voice said again, in her mind.

"Shut up!" she blurted and blushed when she realized she had said it aloud.

"Shut up?" Damian chuckled and then he stretched his hand and with one long, well-manicured finger, pushed a strand of hair off her eyes. "I love your hair, it looks good with your brown skin tone, like dark chocolate on a caramel cake."

"Thank you." Sandy blushed even more.

"I will be here by six to pick you up. We would have dinner before going to the Karaoke bar." Damian leaned forward and bent towards her face.

"Oh my God, he is going to kiss me. I think I am going to faint." The thoughts whirled in her head.

Her eyes closed as she anticipated the kiss, but she felt his mouth brush lightly, inches away from her mouth.

"Look pretty for me," Damian said and walked away.

Chapter Three

⸺⊰⊱⸺

The little lacy black dress made Sandy feel beautiful. This evening she decided to wear her hair up, therefore her black hair was pulled up in a tight ponytail that accentuated her cheekbones and secured with a flowery ribbon. She opted for a simple dash of makeup because she wanted Damian to see her for who she was.

"If he likes me, it has to be the real me he likes," she thought as she swiped a red lipstick on her lips.

She just finished dressing up when her phone rang. Her heart skipped a beat when she saw Damian's name as the caller ID. She took the call and tried as much as she could, to keep the excitement out of her voice.

"I am outside your apartment," Damian said and hung up.

Sandy all but ran down the flight of stairs to the front of the apartment building where she saw the familiar silver BMW. She breathed out and then walked slowly to the car. When she got into the car, Damian turned to take a good look at her. Without saying a word, he stretched his hand and pulled off the flowery ribbon holding her hair up, and her black mane cascaded down her back.

"I told you how much I love your hair and I want to be able to run my hands in them," Damian said with a cocky smile and then he winked at her.

Sandy could swear she heard her heart beating so fast as it would burst out of her chest. Whatever charm Damian had cast on her, it was working.

Throughout their ride out, they did not say a word to each other. Yet, the silence was not uncomfortable. It felt like they enjoyed their company, without necessarily filling it up with a conversation. First, Damian took her to dinner in one of the upscale restaurants in the city. Sandy had a seafood dish for the first time and she loved it. Damian kept picking things off his plate and putting it in her mouth. He was so affectionate, that it was almost unbelievable to think they had known each other for only a day. After dinner, they drove for a short while before the car stopped in front of a bar; it was the Pulse Karaoke bar at Times Square.

"I will do everything to make sure you have a memorable night," Damian said as he took her hand. They walked into the karaoke bar for a night of fun.

At the bar, they had fun, as Damian serenaded Sandy with 'Moonlight Sonata' from Beethoven. While Sandy enjoyed her favorite cherry drink, Damian went for his favorite, the Sour Mash Kentucky bourbon. Sometimes, Sandy found herself staring up into his eyes. Despite the warning bells in her head, telling her that he was way out of her league, she pressed on, opening her heart like flower petals to the morning sun.

"You have amazing eyes," Damian said as he leaned into her. He used a finger and traced her pert nose.

His breath was a sweet mixture of the bourbon, cinnamon from the sweet cake they had after dinner, and peppers from the dinner they ate. Just as the first time they met, she felt her legs go weak. She was grateful that this time she was not standing. However, she stumbled forward into him, and their lips met.

They both froze, with their lips on each other. Then Damian slowly pressed on her lips and pushed them apart. His tongue glided in and invaded her mouth. She tasted him, and all the nerves of her body became aflame. She found herself pressing into him, wishing for more than his tongue. They did not mind that there were others in the bar, as they savored each other's mouth.

"I want you, Sandy," Damian said. But then, he ended the kiss abruptly, pushing her away softly.

"You should come to Rem Energy tomorrow, so you can resume your duties. You would be my assistant." Damian chuckled. "I don't know your qualification, but you can always scale up, depending on your qualifications."

"What!" Sandy was surprised. How did they go from a kiss to that? The warning bells were louder in her ears.

"Why are you surprised?" Damian asked, with a smirk. He knew the effect he had on her. But she was not the only one feeling it. If he had his way, he would be peeling that lacy dress off her and... He shook his head to stop his train of thought.

"Just like that. Won't there be an interview or something?"

"No, I have the right to appoint any staff for myself and I don't need an interview to know you would perform your duties excellently," Damian said.

In that moment of passion, they did not see a man sitting in the shadows and taking pictures of their passionate moment.

The drive back to Sandy's apartment was another silent one. Each of them was immersed in their thoughts. Sandy was falling faster than she had ever fallen for anyone, but she knew she had to fight it. He could just be looking to sleep with her and move on, she told herself.

"I will not let him have his way with me, no matter how fond of him I am becoming." Sandy resolved in her heart as she stole glances at him. He looked deep in thoughts and Sandy wondered what he was thinking about. He was surely the king of mixed signals and she was bad at decoding signals.

When they got on the road that led to her apartment, a shrill sound disturbed the ambiance of the car. Sandy looked just in time to see that Damian's phone was ringing, and the caller ID was a woman named Nicole.

It did not help her insecurities that he refused to take the call. Instead, he switched off the phone. When they got to her apartment, Sandy was almost in tears; she felt everything she had experienced with Damian had all been a waste. She pushed open the door and jumped out of the car. But before she got into the apartment building, Damian went after her and grabbed her. He held her against the wall and crashed his lips on her. All her anxieties disappeared as she leaned in and returned the kiss.

"I have never wanted anyone the way I want you. It is strange, but I like it," Damian said against her mouth. "However, things are complicated and it all revolves around my family."

"What is it about?" Sandy asked, short of breath from kissing.

"You will not understand, even if I explain. It is late already, and you need to be punctual. I will send a driver to get you by eight in the morning." He brushed a light kiss on her forehead and waited until she was safely ensconced in her apartment before leaving.

Lucia Remington was a powerful woman, not only because she was married to the rich and powerful, Carl Remington, but because of the influence she wielded in New York. She was on the board of several companies, including film production companies. At fifty-five, she did not look a day older than thirty-five, with her buxom, yet well-trimmed figure and her face that screamed blue blood. Her light green eyes could make a man pee in his pants if they were directed at him.

Lucia was indeed born into wealth, as her family had a dynasty called Callahan Atlanta. They were the richest family in Atlanta and when they had sought to spread into New York, they had sought out an acquaintance, Carl Remington Snr. He had brokered the marriage between his son and the Callahan daughter, Lucia. The marriage had been stormy, especially with Carl's philandering, but it had been beneficial to both families. It was for this reason that Lucia decided to arrange a profitable marriage for her son Damian. No one was more suitable than Nicole Walton. She had dated her son in the past, and she had come to like her because she saw her young self in her.

Lucia looked at her gold watch again and shook her head in disappointment.

"These young people know nothing about being punctual," she said with derision. She invited Nicole for a chat, but the latter was a few minutes late.

Standing from the chaise in the East balcony, Lucia went to lean on the banister. This position gave her a good view of the Remington manor, a gigantic mansion that was the most talked about in New York.

"All these would belong to my son one day and that is enough consolation for me," Lucia thought, even as her fist clenched involuntarily.

Having just found out about a big family secret, it was time to move swiftly and secure her son's future. She had never loved Carl, as theirs had been a brokered marriage, but still, she wished he had given more to their marriage. No one would stand in the way of her plans to get Damian married to Nicole, not even her son.

Not long afterward, the butler brought Nicole to her. The gorgeous, curvaceous blonde woman sashayed to where Lucia was standing and hugged her.

"It has been a while, ma'am," Nicole said.

"Yes, and I have missed you in all that time. We were a great team," Lucia replied.

When Nicole and Damian were an item, she had many projects with Lucia, especially for women and children. It was the reason Lucia fought against any woman who came into Damian's life after he broke up with Nicole.

"I called you here because I want you to be married to my son." Nicole signaled to the butler. She was ready for dinner.

The kitchen staff brought in trays after trays of food and stood behind for the two beautiful women to have dinner.

"How do you feel about what I have said?" Lucia asked.

"My relationship with Damian broke down because we drifted apart. I don't see how we can go from that to marriage," Nicole replied.

"We can make that happen. I have an idea." Lucia conversed with Nicole in low tones. The more they talked, the wider Nicole's smile became.

"It is a good plan, ma'am Lucia." Nicole clinked her glass with Lucia's as they sealed their deal.

Chapter Four

Sandy could hardly sleep all night. She had heard about the butterflies in the stomach effect, but never really felt it until now. It was only at three in the morning she could finally doze off, after imagining what it would be like, working beside Damian all day.

It was the traffic that woke her. She jumped out of bed at the same time she saw the bedside clock. It was already 7:30; she had only thirty minutes to prepare for her first day at Rem Energy. She chose black pant trousers and paired it with a chiffon blouse and a jacket. When the driver came, she was ready, but that meant she looked plain and uninteresting on her first day. She had no time to work on her hair and so she had put it in a tight bun. Her face was only moisturized and was bare of makeup. If she had known what was waiting for her at Rem Energy, she would have taken more care with her appearance.

When the car pulled into Rem Energy, Sandy was attacked with nerves. The gigantic state-of-the-art building did nothing to give her confidence. It was made worse when she found that Damian was not waiting for her. Navigating her way to the lobby, she went to the front desk, where a redhead sat peering intensely at a computer screen.

"Hello, sorry to bother you, but if you would please point me in the direction of Damian's office," Sandy said.

The receptionist looked at her skeptically, taking in her cheap clothes and bare face. If Damian had not left a message to this effect, she would have thought she was one of the jobless applicants who came to ask her questions about vacancies in the company.

"Are you Miss Sandy?" the receptionist asked.

"Yes, I am and when you are done checking out my clothes, you can point me in the direction I should go," Sandy replied testily.

Sandy got the directions to Damian's office and went on her way. As she came out of the elevator, she bumped into Lucia Remington, Damian's mother, but she did not know this. She got to the office which she had to access through the elevator and knocked twice on the door. When she opened the door, she was greeted with a sight she did not expect. Damian was seated behind his desk, but a blonde was sitting on his table and they were in a deep conversation.

She cleared her throat to announce her presence. When Damian looked up and saw her, an expression came on his face that Sandy could not decipher.

"Just as I told you and my mother, I already have a personal assistant and here she is," Damian said.

The blonde woman turned abruptly as her eyes as golden as a summer sky narrowed. Sandy felt intimidated in her presence, but she was at least grateful that she had put some thought into her appearance before coming. After taking a long look at Sandy, the blonde woman flung her hair and walked to the couch where her bag was. Sandy could not help but envy her trimmed body, which rivaled Kim Kardashian's, without the overly big butt.

"Damian, I will see you at the family dinner," the blonde said and left.

"So where do I start?" Sandy asked, even though she was confused inside.

"Won't you ask me who she is?" Damian asked.

"Is it my business?" Sandy retorted. She wanted to know, but she did not know if she was supposed to ask. They had been on only two dates if she could count the coffee shop.

"But he kissed me," she thought, while her lips remained clamped.

"She is my ex and my mother wanted her to work here, but I already gave you the spot." He sounded like he wanted Sandy to be grateful for that.

"If she is your ex, why is she attending your family dinner?" Sandy could not help but ask.

"She is also a family friend. She and my mother have been on several projects together," Damian replied.

It was a loud warning flag, but Sandy felt helpless; she needed the job to make something of her life. She could not continue relying on her girlfriends. But staying at this job would make her more vulnerable. She and Damian were classes apart and even if he liked her, it was not anything permanent.

"I should be running as far as my legs can carry me, not accepting this job," Sandy thought, but her financial needs won over her emotional needs.

It has been three months since Sandy started working at Rem Energy and in those three months, instead of running away from Damian, she ran towards him. He officially asked her to be his girlfriend after convincing her that there was nothing between him and Nicole.

At that time, they had been on several dates. Damian was the most romantic person Sandy ever met. He set updates in the most creative places. They had a date on a private jet, which went nowhere but fly over New York. It was on the private jet that they made love for the first time. Damian's hand elicited feelings in places she did not even know existed. She climaxed staring down at the skylines of New York City. The feeling was surreal. They had traveled out of the city on dates, and in three months, Sandy spent the night in cities she never thought she would go and dined in places she only saw in movies. But all these did not go unnoticed.

One day, Sandy had just come home from the office and had a date night with Damian later in the evening. She had just undressed and was going to the bathroom to soak in the bathtub when her phone rang. Knowing it could be important, she went back to her bedroom to take the call. She was surprised to find it was her mother.

"Hello, mother," Sandy said.

"Did you forget you have a family in OK? What is this I hear that you are dating a billionaire heir?" Her mother began. "How is it that you have such a rich boyfriend and yet have not sent any money home?"

"Mother, why exactly did you call?" Sandy was not prepared for her mother's tantrums.

"I called to tell you that a man does not take you seriously until he has visited your family. If he wants you permanently, he would come to see your family.

Sandy was still mad at her mother for all the taunts and how everyone including her family walked all over her because she was broke and unmarried. However, she could not deny the fact that her mother was right.

Later that evening while they were out on a date, Sandy brought up the issue of meeting her parents.

"Will you come to Oklahoma with me this weekend?" Sandy asked.

"Why, what is happening there?"

"I want you to meet my parents," Sandy replied, and she saw Damian stop.

"No, I can't this weekend." Damian did not even look at her.

"When can you?" Sandy asked and noticed that Damian was becoming uncomfortable.

"There is a lot on my plate now, so I can't say," Damian replied.

Sandy buried her head in her food as she interpreted the situation. "What exactly do you want from me?"

"Sandy, where is this coming from?" Damian looked up at her.

"Is this a committed relationship or is this just a fling?" Sandy asked, but Damian had no answers. He could not answer because he did not know the answers. He had been avoiding the elephant in the room, and now it was time to face the problem.

When Damian lay in bed that night, he thought of the questions Sandy had asked. He could not take Sandy to his parents because she had no pedigree, but at the same time, he could not let her go. He did not know when it happened, but Sandy had become a major part of his life. They were good together in bed and out of it. But, his family would never accept her. He knew he needed to come to a decision soon, but that did not mean it was an easy decision to make. He was caught between a woman he wanted in his life and his duty to family.

He took out his phone to call Sandy; and stopped himself; she had not said a word to him after they had that conversation and when he took her to her apartment, she only said bye, without even turning to look at him.

He needed to decide, and he needed to make it fast.

"Am I ready to let go of everything for a woman? Is this what they call love?" Damian said to the walls of his bedroom.

At first, Lucia paid no mind to the fledgling romance between her son and Sandy. She had watched him date many women intensely and then dump them like hot potatoes. So, she attributed this to an employee sleeping with her boss. But she became worried when it passed the one-month mark and even became three months. She decided to do something about it.

Sandy was in the office one afternoon going over files Damian needed for a business meeting in the evening. Since that date night where she asked him to visit Oklahoma, she had kept a distance between her and Damian. It was not easy, and she knew it was a temporary solution, especially as her body always betrayed her when Damian was near. His cologne was enough to send memories rushing at her; memories that made it harder for her to keep her distance. Many times, Damian had tried talking to her, but Sandy always rebuffed him

That afternoon, Damian had gone out of the office and unknown to Sandy, he was meeting with Nicole at a spa club. The door opened suddenly, and Lucia Remington walked in. Her presence was intimidating, but Sandy tried not to cower.

"So, you are the girl I hear has been sleeping around shamelessly with my son?" Lucia asked, even though she was not expecting an answer.

"Good day ma'am." Sandy stood up from her seat.

"There is nothing good about the day when your classlessness stinks from miles away." Lucia walked up to her and gave her the stare that made even men quiver. "Whatever you have with my son should end today. You have had the experience of your life and that should be enough. Do not be ambitious, because you are going to hurt yourself."

Sandy was angry, but her nerves failed her, as she remained mute. Lucia circled her as a predator would do a prey.

"Perhaps he did not tell you...of course he wouldn't, not until he is done with you anyway, but he is in a committed relationship with Nicole," the matriarch of the Remington household said.

"That's a lie!" Sandy blurted. Then she caught herself and looked away. "I mean, there is nothing between Damian and the lady."

"What makes you so sure?" Lucia burst into a raucous laugh. "Oh, poor you...I see you have not yet learned the ways of men. Men will tell you anything until they no longer need you. Right now, my son is with Nicole at a spa club. If that is not proof, then I can get you more."

Sandy dropped her eyes because she did not want Lucia to see the hurt in them. Damian told her he was going to the plant, but instead, he was out with Nicole.

"You got fooled again. When are you ever going to learn?" Sandy berated herself inwardly. She felt broken because she had begun to hope. She had never said the L word to Damian, but she knew in her heart she was falling in love with him.

"No, I will not let this woman see me fall apart," Sandy said to herself.

"Thanks for the information, but it is not needed." Sandy turned and walked away.

"I hope I never see your pathetic face again," Lucia said after her.

Sandy did not know where she was going; she only knew she had to leave Rem Energy fast. She rushed out of the elevator into the lobby. As the automatic door opened to let her out, she bumped into Damian, who was walking in with Nicole.

Sandy looked at him with glassy eyes wet with tears and all her feelings for him showed at that moment. She shook her head as the tears began to fall and ran away.

"Sandy!" Damian called after her and ran to catch up with her.

In her haste to get away, Sandy stumbled on to the road and was hit by a car. The moment she fell on the asphalt floor, she remembered crashing into Damian, the first time they met.

"Sandy!" Damian screamed and ran to her.

Sandy was sprawled on the floor, with blood pooling at the back of her head. Damian and the driver of the car ran to her and knelt beside her.

"Sandy, come on, open your eyes." Damian wanted to shake her, but he knew it could only make things worse. "I love you! I love you, Sandy."

His eyes were filled with fear and they glimmered with tears. Nicole stood by the curb and watched everything. She knew Damian so well and could not deny, even if she wanted, that he had fallen in love with Sandy.

"I have to do something fast...before it is too late," she thought within, as she took out her phone and called Lucia Remington.

Chapter Five

Damian had not slept a wink all night; alone in the hospital hall, he had time to reflect on his life and what he had with Sandy. For three months he had been happy with a woman who did not care about his surname or his wealth. He saw how her eyes twinkled when he was close and how different emotions played on her face when they talked. Even though she carried her gait with gentleness, she was full of passion; a fire burned within her and it needed an escape.

His thoughts made him restless; he could not sit still again. Standing up, he walked down to the hospital's cafeteria. At that time of night, there were only a few resident doctors in the cafeteria, so Damian ordered a cup of coffee and sat down alone with his thoughts.

"I told her I loved her...did I say it because I was scared?" Damian thought as he traced the rim of the coffee cup, with one finger.

He had been in love once, but he could not tell what he felt for Sandy. He only knew that at that moment when the car hit her, his life suddenly became too hard to live; like he could not exist if Sandy was not there.

"You are crazy! She is not oxygen. You can live without her," his inner voice told him.

"I can't. I want Sandy in my life," he said aloud.

He lied to Sandy and went to the spa with Nicole because he knew that Sandy could never fit into the kind of life he had. So, he agreed with his mother to rekindle his relationship with Nicole. But all through he watched his phone waiting for Sandy's call. All the time he was with Nicole, he reminisced on his dates with Sandy; her soft laughter, her dancing eyes, her hair which always got into her eyes, the way she blew her hair out of her face instead of sweeping it away with her hands, and even the way she said, 'Kiss me'. The more time he spent at the spa with Nicole, the more he missed Sandy. He just wanted to get back to the office and wrap her in his arms. But obviously, his mother had been up to her tricks and everything had come crumbling down.

"How can I convince her to trust me again?" Damian said in a low tone. Then he started the chair, as an idea lit him up. "Yes, I am going to let her know it is her I want, even though my family may never accept her."

Sandy woke up with a start and was arrested with the feeling of *Deja vu*. It felt like the first time she met Damian; she woke up on a bed in his house, only that this time, it did not look like she was in a house. She looked around her and only realized she was in the hospital when the smell of chlorine, disinfectants, and drugs hit her. Then it all came back to her. She remembered getting hit by a car, but before that incident, she also remembered Lucia Remington, Nicole Walton, and Damian Remington.

"You have stayed long in Lala land. It is time to come back to your senses," Sandy said through clenched teeth.

Just then, the door opened, and the male doctor came in. He checked her eyes and her vital signs. After making his report in Sandy's file, he grinned at her.

"You gave us quite a scare. It is good to see you are recovering. You had a concussion at the back of the head, but we are glad it did not affect any vital centers in the brain. You do remember your name and who you are?"

Sandy looked away as tears began to pool in her eyes. She wished she could forget that once again, she had leaped before she looked. She wished she could forget the words Lucia had said to her.

"Sandy?" the doctor began when she remained quiet. "That's your name, right?"

"Yes, doctor. I haven't lost my memories," Sandy replied, without turning. She would not allow another man to see her cry, even if he was her doctor. She was tempted to go and twitter and tweet the hashtag '#menarescum'.

"Your boyfriend will be happy to hear that. He has been here all night and only went away this morning to freshen up," the doctor explained.

"Her boyfriend?" Sandy pondered in her head. "Was Damian here all night?"

She scoffed, not ready to allow that sway her stance. The first thing she would as soon as she left the hospital was to tender her resignation from Rem Energy. It was time to move on; it had been too good to be true anyway.

The doctor wrote some instructions in the pad for the nurse attendant and turned to leave. But then the door opened and in came a band of guitarists dressed as cowboys. They were playing her favorite, 'Riders in the Sky' and it brought smiles to her face. They came closer and she began to move her legs to the song. The last thing on her mind was who had sent them to serenade her. Then she noticed that one of the cowboys was walking closer to her.

"Sandy, will you marry me?" The cowboy took off his hat and went on his knees.

Sandy's mouth fell open as she saw it was Damian; the hat had obscured his face. She was still lost for words when he took out a box. Her heart almost gave out when he opened it and her eyes rested on a big pink diamond ring.

"That is no way the Sotheby's Pink Star, is it?" Sandy's eyes were wide open in shock.

"It is...I made calls," Damian replied, but instead of being impressed, Sandy was reminded of how unlikely they were. He could make calls and buy one of the world's costliest diamond ring. Who was she kidding? Love did not cross boundaries.

"You should be giving that ring to Nicole. She is the one who fits into your nice, little family. As for me, I am done being in fantasy land." Sandy started to turn her back on him, but he wrapped his arms around her.

"I do not know when you became so important to me...I do not know when you became my oxygen, but I can't let you walk out of my life. I love you, Sandy. It took you getting hit by a car and seeing you sprawled in your blood, to realize that I love you." Damian looked deep into her eyes, even as she searched his for the truth.

"What about Nicole...what about your mom?" Sandy asked.

"I will handle them. All I want is for you to be mine, forever." Damian took out the ring and with his eyes, he asked Sandy again, if she would marry him.

"Yes, I will!" Sandy wrapped her arms around his neck, as tears cascaded down her cheeks.

Damian slipped the ring on her finger and then he slowly took her mouth in his. While he did this, the guitar band played songs for them. Sandy's heart busted with love for Damian.

"Did I ever tell you?" Sandy asked.

"Tell me what?" Damian's brows were furrowed in puzzlement.

"I love you, Damian. I never thought I would ever say this to anyone. I came to New York a broken girl who had lost at life and love. But today, I see you and I cannot wait to live forever with you," Sandy replied and then nibbled on his lower lip.

Sandy was discharged the next day and Damian took her home. Her friends suggested Damian brought her to Hailey's house, so she could be taken care of, while she recuperated. The first thing the girls saw when Sandy walked in was the big Pink Star.

"Shut up!" Hailey exclaimed.

"Bite me!" Bridget said as she pulled Sandy to the couch.

"Is that the Sotheby's Pink Star?" Spencer asked, with her mouth wide open in shock.

"Hey, girls, please take care of her," he said, unfazed by their reactions. Then he turned to Sandy and brushed a kiss on her cheek. "I will be back to see you...sometime in the evening."

"All right, babe." Sandy kissed him on the mouth before letting him go.

As soon as Damian left, Sandy burst into giggles as her friends congratulated her.

"So, you landed yourself a super-rich fiancé. I am so happy for you," Hailey said and they all piled on Sandy, giving her a bear hug. Sandy could not wait to break the news to her family, but she restrained herself. Instead of telling them over the phone, she would take Damian to Oklahoma to see her family. She wanted to see their faces when she told them she was getting married. However, things would not go as she planned; in fact, they would be so wrong.

"What have I done? I cannot imagine life without her, but am I ready to go toe to toe with my family?" Damian pondered as he navigated his way home. He could have gone to the Remington manor, but he chose his house. He would avoid his mother for as long as he could.

When he pulled into his driveway, he was surprised to find Nicole's red sports car parked. He got out of his car with hurried steps and walked into the house. When he came in, there was no one in the living room, but the house smelled good. Someone had made his favorite chilaquiles. The pungent flavor of the cilantro made him know that whoever was in his kitchen had made the chilaquiles just the way he liked it; with feta, onions, and cilantro. With tentative steps, he walked towards the kitchen. When he pulled open the door, he found Nicole dressed in a lace romper and dancing in front of the gas cooker.

"Nicole?" Damian said, with surprise on his face. She stopped dancing and turned to him with a smile.

"Welcome home. I was surprised to find that you still left your key under the doormat...a pleasant surprise anyways," Nicole flashed him a pregnant look.

"What are you doing?" Damian started. "Before we decided to go our separate ways years ago, we agreed we were not compatible. You had a love interest too...what was his name again...Lance!"

"I thought you were all right with what your mother wanted. You took me to the spa and you said, perhaps we were made for each other. What were you doing then?" Anger flashed in Nicole's eyes. She had seen Damian give up on the fling he had with Sandy, but that accident had somehow made him attached to her. She wished Sandy had died instead.

"I was confused. But after almost losing Sandy, I realized that I am in love with her," Damian replied. "You know I don't have feelings for you."

"Who cares about that? What can she possibly give you?" Her fingers were clenched, and she was losing control over her emotions.

"She loves me and that is enough!" Damian yelled and walked away. He did not like where the conversation was going.

Nicole went after him, dumping the kitchen mitts on the kitchen table. Lucia had told her to push him because Damian did not respond well to pressure. All she hoped for, was one mistake that would push Sandy out of his life for good.

"Damian! What can love do for you? Love does not build legacies and dynasty. We don't need a puppy love, Damian. We have passion, we have a family name. Together we can build a dynasty... just think about how we would rule the world together." As she said this, she edged closer to him and even though his back was turned to her, she glided her arms around his waist and pulled him to her.

Slowly, she nibbled his ear-lobe, working her way upward, leaving hot kisses in her wake. Every place she kissed became excited, as Damian was reminded of what it used to be like, with Nicole; their relationship had been more of fiery passion than love. Nicole could tell Damian's resolve was failing him; no man had ever been able to resist her, not even Damian. Slowly she turned him to face her and then she looked deep into his eyes.

"Think of what we can accomplish together. The kind of life we would live and how much we would make our families happy. You once told me that family is always first and now you know, that your family will never accept her." Nicole splayed her fingers on his chest and slowly removed his shirt. "Your father will be disappointed."

Damian could not think straight. He loved Sandy, but it did not mean that Nicole was wrong. He wondered what he would do if push came to shove. Could he sacrifice his family's wealth and name for love? He tried to get out of Nicole's hold, as he filled his mind with thoughts of Sandy, but the more he pushed, the more she held on to him. He had never seen this side of her; her eyes burned with desire, turning its golden color into an almost amber hue.

"Nicole..." Damian said weakly, even as Nicole crushed his lips with hers.

"I have waited so long for this. You are mine, Damian, and I am never going to let you go," Nicole said against his lips. "I made that mistake once, but I won't repeat it."

Damian's desires overrode his resolve and he found himself pushing Nicole towards the bedroom. With a hunger for her, he peeled the romper away from her body, shredding it into several pieces. He carried a naked Nicole and suspended her against the wall. He did not know when his desires turned into anger; he was angry at her for being his mother's weapon against his relationship with Sandy. He was angry at his weakness and for not being firm in his decision to stick to Sandy.

"Do you know that I am engaged to Sandy? I bought her the Sotheby's Pink Star and asked her to marry me," Damian said as he roughly plunged into her. He pounded into her with all his pent-up frustration.

"This is what you wanted, isn't it? You wanted to test my resolve, didn't you?" he pounded into her with reckless abandon.

"Stop! You are hurting me." Nicole was no longer feeling pleasure but pain. The heated sex did nothing to mask the disgust on Damian's face. "Let me go!"

Nicole slapped Damian hard across the face and he let her go. She ran into the toilet to cry her eyes out. She had gotten what she wanted, at a high cost. Damian had not made love to her, he had used her. A bitter smile came across her tear-stained face. "I have gotten what I wanted, Damian and by God, you will do right by me," she thought.

Chapter Six

S andy did not get a call in the evening from Damian, but she did not want to appear clingy, so she spent the evening with Hailey, Bridget, and Spencer, as they had a pajamas party, with cakes, wine, and gossip.

The next morning, she woke up, she knew she had to return to the office as she did not want to act privileged just because she was engaged to the Remington heir.

"You are not going to get any reasonable cloth from your wardrobe at home, so just use one of Hailey's," Bridget said, as they all got ready to go back to their busy lives.

"Don't insult me." Sandy feigned anger.

Nevertheless, she took Bridget's advice and borrowed one of Hailey's blue, wide-legged, pant trouser suit. She pulled her hair up in a tight bun to accentuate her face and she applied natural makeup. As Sandy dressed up, she thought of the incoming storm. She did not deceive herself into thinking that everything was going to be all right, because she knew it would not, at least at first.

"For one, Lucia will not accept the marriage, neither will his father," Sandy thought.

"What did you say?" Sandy turned abruptly and saw Hailey in the bedroom where she was dressing up.

"I said that aloud?" Sandy retorted.

"Yes," Hailey replied and looked at her with concerned eyes. "I know you are worried about your relationship with Damian. Have faith that everything will turn outright. The most important thing is that you both love each other because love conquers all."

"Thank you, Hailey...I don't know what I would have done without you." Sandy pulled Hailey into a hug.

Nicole closed the door of her executive office at Walton Corp and took out her phone. She had been busy having a teleconference with their staff at the Atlanta branch and sending a videotape to a celebrity talk show. She needed to update Lucia Remington, so she took out her phone and started dialing.

"Nicole, tell me it is done," Lucia said, picking up at the first ring.

"It is. I am sure it is going to push that desperate woman out of his life for good," Nicole replied.

"Remember what I told you; blame me, because Damian can never stay angry at me, but it could spoil any chances of you both getting together if he finds out you had a hand in it."

"All right ma'am. Thanks for all your help. When Damian and I broke up, I never thought we had a future together anymore, but you have given me hope," Nicole said.

"I am doing this for my family...." Lucia let her voice trail off.

"You never told me what the big secret was you found out about your family," Nicole said.

"That is why it is called a secret. Talk later, I have an empire to run." Lucia hung up abruptly.

"Hmmn..." Nicole became thoughtful, but she did not dwell on it. If she was going to be a member of the family, she was sure she would find out all about their dirty little secrets.

Damian had just entered his office when his phone rang; it was his childhood best friend, Jamie, who worked at a television station. He wanted to ignore the call because he was not in a chatty mood. He was supposed to call Sandy, but he did not even know how he could face her. The guilt was eating him up. On second thought, he decided to pick up the call.

"Hello buddy," he said.

"I don't know what is going on, but your sex tape is with one of our talk show hosts." Jamie dropped the bombshell. "It was sent in this morning. I stumbled in on the viewing..." Jamie sounded uncomfortable, as a straight man would sound after seeing his fellow man's naked body. "I thought you broke up with Nicole."

Damian sat down hard in his chair, with his mouth open in surprise.

"What do I do?" Jamie asked.

"Stop it however you can. Please get me the video and you would be beautifully compensated," Damian said when he found his tongue.

"I will do it, but not for the compensation. What are friends for?" Jamie asked.

"Thank you, bro., I owe you big. Get the tape for me please."

The moment Damian dropped the call, he took his car keys off the table and walked out of his office. In anger, he drove to Walton Corp. where he knew Nicole would be. He ignored greetings from the staff and marched straight to Nicole's office.

"What did you do?" he snarled as he made for Nicole, whose eyes shone with fear. The Damian she knew would never hurt her. But the situation he was in, was getting him frustrated and pressured. A Damian like that could do anything.

Damian gripped both her arms and shook her. "How could you stoop so low?"

"What have I done?" Nicole asked, her eyes filled with fear.

"You came into my house and installed cameras, so you could make a sex tape? What were you trying to do, destroy my relationship with Sandy?"

"I don't know what you are talking about. Why would I make a sex tape? Do you think I would destroy my image for you? I am a businesswoman and the future of Walton Corp. lay on my shoulders. I can't make bad decisions like that."

"Then who?" Damian let go of her arm.

"You should ask your mother. You have made her desperate. She told me that she found out a big secret about your family and wants to protect you," Nicole replied.

Damian became thoughtful and then he walked away, no turning back, despite calls from Nicole.

As Damian drove back to his office, he realized that there could be copies of that videotape and he could not watch his mother's every move. The only solution was to open to Sandy.

"Are you crazy? She will never trust you again," an inner voice chided him.

"What do I do? I do not want to lose Sandy," Damian thought. Then a light bulb went on in his head.

He was engaged to Sandy and there was no reason to wait on getting married. He decided he would whisk Sandy away to her hometown and marry her there.

"She would love it. She has always wanted me to see her parents. It would be a beautiful surprise wedding," Damian said with excitement.

Lucia had hoped the plan would work to drive Sandy away from her son's life, and then she would not have cared about Damian's wrath. But the plan had failed and now that her son knew she was responsible, she could not do anymore, even though she had extra tapes. It would irk her son and she did not want to alienate him.

"But there is something I can do. Now, I must be subtle, and to win my enemy, I must bring her closer," Lucia thought with a wicked grin, as she danced her fingers over the rim of the delicate china teacup.

She was sitting in her garden and just remembered that the annual Remington ball was fast approaching. If she knew her son well, he would invite Sandy; that would her opportunity to sabotage her and take her away for good. Excited over her new plans, she drops the teacup and beckons for the driver to take her out to Rem Energy. On the drive there, she calls her stylist to get her a dress that said, 'Matriarch in control.' On that day, she would be intimidating two people with her outfit, her son's wretched lover, and her husband's mistress.

Sandy came out of the elevator and walked right into Lucia Remington. Her eyes flashed with anger before she smiled; a smile that did nothing to convince Sandy or relax her nerves. No matter how hard she tried, she always felt the need to cower in Lucia's presence. She wished the woman would accept her, after all, they were going to be a family.

"Hi, Sandy," Lucia said, looking at Sandy's cashmere dress. She could see her fashion sense had improved since the last time they met, courtesy of her son's money. She wanted to show her disgust, but that would not be good for her plans.

"Ma'am...sorry for walking into you...I" Sandy stuttered.

"Do not worry your little head, you are just the person I was looking for." Lucia swept her hair to the side and fixed her intimidating gaze on Sandy. "You are an important part of my son's life and I think we should find a common ground where we can relate. I think shopping would be the best place to start...every woman loves to shop."

"Thanks for the gesture, ma'am. But I do not need to shop," Sandy replied with a nervous smile.

"You do need to shop because you need clothes. You must have heard about the Remington ball, more like a retreat held annually and I am sure Damian would want you to come." Lucia smiled sweetly, even though it took all her resolve not to snarl at Sandy for turning down her offer in the first place.

"All right, ma'am. When..."

"Now." Lucia did not let Sandy finish. "Come on, my driver is waiting."

"No, no, no, wait...where are you taking her?" Damian rushed to them. He had seen Sandy walking away with his mother and expected the worst.

"Relax son, one would think I want to harm her or something. We are only going shopping," Lucia said and patted her son on the cheek.

"Why?" Damian looked panic-stricken. All he could think of was the duplicate videotapes which he knew his mother must-have. His mother made copies of everything.

"You must have forgotten the Remington ball, but I did not, and I want your lover to uphold the standards of the Remington name, seeing as she is an important part of you." Lucia turned to Sandy and beckoned her to follow her.

Unknown to them, Nicole had put a tail in the person of the doorman who listened to every exchange, so he could relay to his boss. Later, he would tell Nicole everything and she would become worried, so much that she would put around the clock tail on Sandy and everyone connected to her. Whatever Damian was planning with her, she wanted to be the first to know, so she could stop it.

Chapter Seven

⟡

The Remington ball was an annual event hosted by the Remington family in celebration of their business partners, friends, and well-wishers. At the ball, the elite of the society gathered to play chess, horse race, network, sign business deals, and party all night. It was a three-day event and always held at the Remington Ranch house, a large castle little settlement spanning hectares and hectares of land.

This year's ball was no different as everyone that mattered in the society came out to play and party with the Remington's. Hailey, Bridget, and Spencer helped Sandy get ready for the event; they had arranged her clothes with labels, according to the days she would wear them. The clothes were from the most luxurious clothing brands because Lucia had paid for them. There were clothes for the horse racing event, a designer one-piece swimsuit for the poolside party and of course a ball gown for the ball party. At 5 pm, Damian came to pick up Sandy, and together they went to the Remington ranch in the Hampton.

Remington did not disappoint as there was so much fun to be had. Sandy had never in her life been in such a party; it was as if she could become rich just by being at the party. The caliber of people in the party was the type she never dreamed of staying with, under the same roof.

It was the second day of the retreat which saw the horse race competition. This year, the Remington horse did not win, but a man whom nobody knew. He was called Hector and he was a handsome, proud man, with long brown hair which he tied behind his head and same brown eyes as Damian's. Because no one knew him, they assumed he was also an elite, for him to have entered the ranch. Later in the evening, there was scheduled a group dinner, which would award a title belt to the winner of the horse race. Unknown to Sandy, something had been planned for that evening. Sandy felt pressed from eating too much. It seemed that one of the waiters was commissioned by Damian to pump her with food.

"Is he trying to fatten me before the wedding?" Sandy thought. "Where is he anyway?"

She had not seen Damian since that evening but believed he was busy with corporate duties, because an event like this could not go without signing business deals and networking.

"I should go to the restroom. I would empty my bowels and stay away from the crowd for a few minutes," Sandy thought and walked out of the dining hall in the direction of the restroom.

In the restroom, Sandy emptied her bowels as she intended and tried to freshen her look. She was looking into the mirror when she heard the door open and a man walked in. She was still wondering if it was a unisex restroom when the man grabbed her breasts from behind.

"What are you doing?"

"Do not lie, you want me. I saw you look at me all evening. Come on," the man said kissing her neck. He turned her forcefully and buried his lips in her face, smearing her makeup on him. Then he yanked the front of her buttoned-down dress and pulled out a few buttons, leaving the top of her breasts bare.

"Say it! You want me," he rubbed himself against her and moaned loudly.

All the while, Sandy whimpered as she struggled against him. "Let me go, I beg of you."

"I won't, not until I am done," the man replied, even though he did not attempt to do undress her.

Back in the dining hall, Lucia rushed to her husband, looking flustered and scared. "Where is Damian, we need to avert a problem. A staff just told me something is going on in one of the restrooms. I see scandal brewing if this is rape or murder."

"Rape? Murder? That has never happened before," Carl said, with confusion on his face. He was just a few hours away from closing the biggest deal in their business life and he needed no scandals. He beckoned to Damian and appraised him of the situation. They called a few security guys and went towards the restroom. However, Lucia was not going to allow just a few people to witness what she had planned in the restroom, so she asked her trusted assistant, a loquacious young lady, to spread the word that a thief was caught in the restroom.

When the Remington family got to the restroom, they were surprised to find half of their guests with them. Carl Remington became more worried at this turn of events. He became more worried when he heard moans coming from the restroom. But before they could go in, Sandy stumbles out, looking disheveled. Her hair was all over her face, her makeup was smeared, and her buttons were undone. The man who accosted her in the restroom stumbled out after her. His flap was undone, and his face smeared with makeup. He looked up with a surprised expression and then snickered.

"What, can't a man have random sex with a stranger at this party?" the man asked.

"What rubbish! This is disgusting!" one of the guests said.

"Sandy? What is going on here?" Lucia asked, with a feigned pained look on her face. She looked as though she was disappointed in Sandy.

"It is not what you think...he accosted me..." Sandy could barely get the words out before Lucia silenced her with a slap across the face.

"How could you do this?" Lucia said no further because she had acted enough to convince both Sandy and Damian that she was simply disappointed.

"Who is this and why is she at this party?" Carl asked as anger flashed in her eyes.

"I invited her..." Damian started to say.

Sandy's face lit up because, during the madness which she was finding hard to understand, Damian was going to stand up for her.

"You invited her. Why would you do that?" His father was both confused and angry.

"She is my secretary...I invited her..."

43

"Let's not allow this to spoil our mood. Everyone back to the dining hall," Lucia said, taking control of the situation before Damian said more.

As everyone walked away, Sandy looked at Damian with eyes shimmering with unshed tears. She could not stop her heart from breaking. Damian had told everyone she was his secretary, instead of his fiancée.

"Who am I kidding? How can he marry me when he has not told anyone of our engagement? I am such a fool!" Sandy thought as the tears fell in quick torrent.

"Damian?" Carl turned and called after his son. Damian had no choice but to turn away and leave with his father. Lucia smiled covertly, but Sandy had seen her and knew now that everything that happened, happened because of her.

Nicole had been busy in one of the drawing rooms with a potential investor, and so had not witnessed the humiliation of Sandy. However, Lucia was quick to fill her in, as they sat by the poolside, with flutes filled with champagne.

"You should have seen her face! I almost pitied her," Lucia said. "If only she was not standing in the way of my goals for Damian."

"I missed the show, but I am still glad. It happened. Now, I hope Damian is repulsed by that, enough to send her packing out of his life," Nicole replied thoughtfully. She could not wait to be married to Damian. Her hands shook as she took a glance at the Remington Matriarch. She had a secret of her own and it was her motivation for marrying Damian.

"Damian will not be a problem. Do you know he denied her when his father asked who she was? He told everyone she was his secretary. I think it would be easy to sway him...just leave everything to me," Lucia said.

"Yes, I will leave everything to you, just until I marry your son. Then you better butt out," Nicole thought.

Sandy sat on a stone bench in the orchard and stared at the star blanketed sky. It was as if she was looking up at the stars for a message. She came to New York to better her life, but the highest she had done is to be engaged to a rich heir, who was not straight with her. He valued his family and possessions over her. He kept stringing her along and yet she stayed.

"I am so foolish," Sandy said aloud into the still night.

"No, you are not," a voice replied behind her.

"Damian!" Sandy's eyes were filled with anger, as she glared at him. "It is good you came, because I have something for you."

Sandy dug the pocket of the shift dress she had changed into and brought out the Pink Star, the ring Damian had engaged her with.

"I should have known better when you told me not to wear it here," Sandy said through clenched teeth.

"You don't understand. I was trying to protect you. The moment they find out we were engaged, you would be shredded into pieces by the public. My mother would spare nothing to destroy you. I wanted to take them by surprise." Damian walked up to her in long strides and wrapped her in his arms. "But now, that won't happen anymore. I will come clean."

"Don't you know by now, how much I love you?" Damian whispered into her hair. "I had planned a surprise wedding for you. I was going to take you to Oklahoma after the ball, so we could be married. But I have thought about us long and hard...while trying to protect you, I cannot lose you."

"I did not know...I thought..." Sandy stuttered, but Damian silenced her with a kiss.

"Here you go." He took the Pink Star from Sandy and slipped it on her finger. "Go up to your room now, and rest. Tomorrow is the grand ball, and by noon I will send people to your quarters. No matter what happens, I will always love you. You know that, right?"

The Remington grand ball came and met the retreaters with anticipation. The grand ball organized by the Remington's was always talked about for at least six months. The day had been busy for Sandy because Damian kept to his words and sent over beauticians who pampered Sandy. They made a movable hot bath with hot stones. They scrubbed every inch of her body until her brown shade shone with a gold hue. Her hair was treated until it was voluminous, black and silky.

On the other side of the suite, beauticians were also in Nicole's room pampering her with the latest in cosmetics. Today, she was going to swing into her plans to take Damian back. She wanted to be the center of attention, cozy up to the people that mattered, including Damian's father, Carl Remington. When it was time for the ball, she was escorted by one of the staff to the ballroom, which swam with bodies dressed in expensive outfits.

"Clearing my account to get this handmade dress was worth it," Nicole thought to herself, as she basked in the attention given to her. Her red Ellie Saab dress was the talk of the guests in the ballroom.

Her heart caught in her chest as she saw Damian walking towards her. However, he did not reach her but walked to the front of the ballroom where a pianist was playing a rendition.

Damian smiled at everyone present in the ballroom, whose eyes were fixed on him. He felt nervous, but he had to do it if he wanted to assure Sandy. He beckoned to the waiter and got a tall flute of sparkling white wine.

"Cheers to everyone who took out time to celebrate with us this year; the old friends, and the new friends. The Remington's appreciate that you share in our happiness. Cheers to my father, Carl Remington, the fastidious entrepreneur, and my mother, the strong woman of the Remington clan." Damian raised his glass to his father and mother.

"No, I want to introduce the latest addition to the Remington clan..." Damian said.

Carl Remington looked up sharply and then he turned back to investigate the crowd of aristocratic faces. Lucia Remington was also taken aback, and she gasped, wondering what her son was on to.

"There is a lady in red, who is not only going to become my lady but a daughter of the Remington family. I would love you to share in my happiness because I have found a woman, whose worth is far above rubies," Damian continued.

Everyone turned to look at Nicole, whose face became lit with a glorious smile. Coincidentally, she was the only woman wearing a red dress and it appears Damian was looking at her. They smiled at Nicole and she smiled back.

"He realized the mistake he was making and knows I am the best for him. Oh my, I thought I was going to work to convince him, but it seems he concluded, all by himself. I cannot believe my luck," Nicole thought as her red bow-shaped lips spread into a wider smile.

"Come, my lady," Damian said, and Nicole started to move.

But the door flung open and a woman in a red dress, not just any red dress, but the costliest dress by Ellie Saab, a tambour beaded dress, embellished with precious stones, which made the dress so heavy. The dress was handmade by a hundred people and took three months to make. It was the same dress Nicole planned to buy for her wedding reception.

People gasped as the woman walked through, towards Damian. She smiled sweetly, and it was only then that Nicole realized it was Sandy all along.

Sandy took Damian's hand and there were more gasps as the ring on her finger caught the light; the Pink Star was unmistakable.

"I asked her to marry me and she said yes. But now, I will ask her in front of everyone. Will you marry me?"

"Yes, I will," Sandy replied.

A few persons who loved love stories clapped, but many of the guests were disgusted with Damian's decision. Some did not forget the scene at the restroom the evening before and they wondered how he could give his name to a scandalous woman. Carl Remington stood up from his seat, looked up at his son, and walked away with angry strides. Nicole was beside herself with anger. She wished she could kill anyone without consequences, then Sandy would be a dead woman. She vowed to serve her the same humiliation she got. As for Lucia, her world was collapsing right before her eyes and she vowed to do anything it took to send Sandy away from her son's life.

She looked at the woman who was staring at her, dressed simply in a black dress; her husband's mistress. She had a half-smile on her face.

She walked up to the woman, taking a good look at her. She realized that her husband had a type; strong, blonde woman, with fiery green eyes. The woman looked almost her age, but Lucia knew this woman was way younger than her

"I know everything, but I would die before I allow you to reap where you did not sow. You can take that to the bank," Lucia said and walked away.

Chapter Eight

After the Remington ball, Sandy became an instant celebrity. They poked into her life, as they looked for scandals or anything they could expose to the public of their new princess. There were pictures of her college days in the newspaper and it was as though she was running for an elective office.

One would think Sandy enjoyed the attention, but she did not. She felt naked and vulnerable and constantly needed reassurance from Damian, that everything was going to be all right. He invited Sandy over to dinner at the manor, so he could properly introduce her to his family. At the manor, Lucia rushed down the stairs because she saw them from her bedroom window.

"Damian, what is she doing here?" Lucia asked.

"You invited Nicole and she is not a member of this family. Sandy here is soon to be my wife...she has every right to be here," Damian replied.

"Damian, I can go..." Sandy said in a small voice.

"Don't act like you are not enjoying all these," Lucia said bitingly.

Just then Carl walked down the staircase. He fixes his gaze on Sandy and then looks at his son. Without a word, he walks straight to the dining table and sits at the head of the table.

"I would like to eat now," he said, and the kitchen staff went into a flurry of activities.

Dinner was quiet, with Carl's continued glances at Sandy, to Lucia's consternation. However, watching her husband's eye Sandy like a prey, she was struck with an idea to get Sandy off her child's back. However, she knew she had to tread carefully, because the last time she tried to sabotage Sandy, Damian went public with their relationship. When dinner ended, Sandy could not wait to leave the manor to her comfortable apartment. But on their way back, she realized Damian was not driving in the direction of her house.

"Damian, where are you going?"

"My house...with all the craziness, I have not spent time with you. Spend the night with me, will you?" Damian looked at her with those eyes that often made her go weak. She wanted to spend the night thinking about her life and her relationship, but in a heartbeat, she accepted to spend the night with Damian.

"How was dinner?" he asked.

"Icy?" Sandy looked out the window as the beautiful city flew past her.

"It is going to get better, as soon as they come to know how amazing you are." Damian laced his hand in his and brought it to his mouth. "Love conquers all, so don't worry."

Damian had planned a special night for them. As soon as they got to his house, he swept her off her feet and took her to the bedroom, where he ran a lavender-scented bath. Together, they soaked in the tub, with a glass of wine on the tub. Damian teased Sandy's ears, licking at the lobes and moving his tongue up. Sandy began to feel hot inside, but she couldn't tell if it was an effect of the wine or what Damian was doing.

"You like it?" he asked.

"Don't stop," Sandy replied with her lips slightly apart.

From her ears, he moved down her neck and grazed it with his teeth. Slowly, he teased her lips further apart with his tongue and dug inside her mouth like he was searching for gold. Sandy felt inflamed and she roamed her hands over Damian's body, looking for an outlet for her desires.

"I have never wanted any woman the way I want you," Damian said as he cupped her breasts with his large hands.

"Not even Nicole?" Sandy asked.

"She has got nothing on you, babe."

With their hearts beating as one, they made love right there in the tub. From the tub, he took her to the bedroom and made love to her again. It seemed like there were new places in her body he was trying to discover. From the bedroom, he took her to the balcony, which overlooked the city. Staring at the city skyline, he thrust into her, with all the love he had to give. As he did, he promised himself he would never give her up, no matter what his family wanted.

"They would oppose me, but they will come around because we are family," he thought.

While this was happening, Carl was in his study taking a phone call, when Lucia walked in. She had her night robe on, but it clung to her naked body, such that Carl could ferret out her form. There was a time he got excited at the sight of her body, not anymore.

"You were talking to her, weren't you?" Lucia said, crossing her arms over her chest.

"Aren't you too old for this kind of jealousy?" Carl retorted.

"I couldn't care less about where you put your thing into. But I want you to know, that I know everything, and I will not allow you to take my son's inheritance away. I was instrumental to what Rem Energy is today and my family was instrumental in making the Remington name what it is today. So, I will not sit by and watch someone reap where they did not sow," Lucia said through clenched teeth.

"Amid your betrayals, I have stayed for my son and I will not allow you to cast him aside. It would be over my dead body. You can tell her that." Lucia turned on her heels and walked away.

It was this encounter in the study that precipitated what Carl did the next morning.

Sandy woke up in Damian's arms with a smile on her face as she thought of the night before. But she sprang up when her eyes rested on the bedside clock. She was going to be late if she did not rush into the bathroom.

"Where do you think you are going?" Damian pulled her back to the bed and imprisoned her with his strong arms around her.

"I am going to be late for work," Sandy protested.

"We should both take the day off." Damian nibbled her neck, causing Sandy to gasp.

"No! I won't be that woman who takes advantage of her relationship. You employed me to do the job, that I will do. Now, I will check in your wardrobe to see if I left a work outfit here." Sandy took to Damian's walk-in closet to check for an outfit to work.

The Walton mansion in Upper East Side stood tall in the morning sun. Inside the house, the Walton family was gathered at the breakfast table. The table was laid out with different dishes; the type you can only find on the table of the wealthy. But the food on the table did not tell the true story.

The true story was, the patriarch of the Walton family, Ben Walton, had brokered a bad deal with money loaned from the bank. The Walton business was in trouble, but they had paid the important people to keep it under wraps, while they still mingled with the wealthiest of New York. Without the board's knowledge, he had taken a huge loan, mortgaging the mansion and the company. Now they had only three months left before the bank foreclosed because their payment was late for up to two years. However, there was a ray of hope when Lucia approached their daughter and asked her to marry her son. It was the perfect opportunity to clear their debts and ride on the good fortune of the Remington's. It was Nicole's motivation in marrying Damian.

"We have only three months to make this work, but he has proposed to another woman. Didn't you say Lucia wanted you to marry Damian?" Ben asked his daughter.

"She has done so many things to get that wretched girl out of Damian's life, but nothing has worked. However, I have another plan, which is going to seal the deal this time." Nicole looked confident, with a cocky smile on her face. "I know Damian is family-oriented and so if he knew his family was on the brink of falling apart, his love for that ratchet girl, would take the back burner."

"I hope you are right, for all our sake," Ben replied, twisting his white chin beards.

"Be careful though, love is a powerful thing. If he loves her, it would be hard to send her away," her mother, Katrina Walton, quipped.

"He loved me once...I will help him remember." Nicole hoped in her heart that she could win this fight, or else, her family was doomed.

Chapter Nine

After a stressful day at the office, Damian decided to have a relaxed night and so he planned a date with Sandy. Under a short period, he could not believe how indispensable she had become. She helped him with his work and wrote the best proposals he had ever seen. She also gave him tips on how to deal with some of his difficult clients. Many times, he had asked her to get an MBA, to increase her potentials, but she always said, "After the wedding, I will."

As Damian got ready for his date night with Sandy, his phone rang. He was excited, thinking it was Sandy. But the smile on his face died when he saw it was his father.

"Hello son, I would like you to come to the manor for dinner. It is important that you do," his father said.

"I am going to have dinner with my fiancé," Damian replied.

"Since meeting that woman, you have become irresponsible." His father's voice was cold, and anger dripped from it. "You are the heir of the Remington dynasty. I did as my father said, to continue the dynasty and make our family stronger. You think when I married your mother I did not have someone I loved. But real men do everything they can for their families."

"You think this way because you believe family advancement can only be through marriage. I will not sacrifice my love for a few business investments," Damian said.

His father kept quiet and after a few moments, hung up the call.

Lucia sat in her bedroom and listened to the conversation between father and son, through the extension. Her palms became sweaty as she listened to her husband's veiled threat. Before she found out the secret, it could have been an empty threat, but now, Lucia knew he would do it. She had a problem with her hands and she knew the solution was at the source.

"That wretched girl! Who gave her the right to tear my family apart? The family I sacrificed all for.... the family I built in the face of betrayal and nights of tears," Lucia said to the empty room.

Slowly, with thoughtful steps, she walked to her dresser and took her phone. She scrolled through her phone until she got to the number she wanted. Staring at the number, she could not help but think about the many times she was tempted to step out on her husband but stayed.

"Mitch is the perfect person for what I have planned," Lucia thought as she dialed the number.

Date night with Sandy was devoid of the fun and happiness they were used to. While Sandy blabbered on about different things just to get Damian to cheer up, the latter looked on morosely. He could not take his mind off the conversation with his father; he always put his family first, but now he was forced, because of his feelings, to go against them.

"Is anything the matter? You have not been yourself since this evening." Sandy took his hand and massaged it. Even though he did not say, she knew it had to do with their relationship.

"When can we go to Oklahoma? I want us to get away from all the stress of this city. I think it is time for me to meet your parents," Damian said.

"Wow! We can go when you are ready." Sandy was excited.

"Let's go tomorrow," Damian said. He told himself it was time to give her that surprise wedding.

The next day, Hailey, Bridget, and Spencer helped Sandy pack. They also packed a bag for themselves. When Sandy asked why they wanted to come to Oklahoma with her, they told her it was for moral support and to get away from New York.

"If we go with you, it is going to be an all-expense-paid trip, so why won't we?" Hailey said.

"It is not like it is to an exotic location, but a getaway is a getaway," Spencer quipped.

Unknown to her, Damian had contacted them and told them of his plan to arrange a surprise wedding in Oklahoma. When they were ready to go, Damian sent a driver to take them to a private airfield, where they would board the Remington private jet.

When Sandy and her friends got to the private airfield, they saw that Damian was already there and talking to the pilot.

"Baby, I am sorry. My friends wanted to come," Sandy said.

"It is all right." Damian pulled her into his arms and kissed her. It was as if with the kiss, he was trying to reassure himself of his decision to go against his family.

The pilot had just given the boarding order when they saw a car approach. When it came closer, Damian saw it was his family's town car. In seconds, Carl Remington came out of the car, fuming with anger.

"If you are going to go against me, then you have no right to any of the family's properties. You are fired from your position at Rem Energy!"

"You cannot do that. I am the heir of the Remington family. Your father did not disinherit you and you cannot do that to me," Damian replied, maintaining his cool.

"Oh really, you watch and see what I am going to do." His father glared at him and in his eyes, there was disappointment, anger, and determination.

"If you remove me from the company or tamper with my inheritance, I will sell the company shares in my possession at a ridiculous price, which would topple Rem Energy." Damian returned his father's glare.

"You would do that?" Carl was surprised.

"Yes, if you go ahead with your threats. I love Sandy, why can't you see that? We do not need marriage to advance the Remington dynasty."

Carl shook his head, disappointed and left. His mind was made up; there was nothing else he could do.

"Come on, let's board now," Damian said as if nothing happened, but Sandy knew better.

On their flight to Oklahoma, after the girls had gotten over their excitement of traveling in a private jet, they called Sandy aside to talk to her.

"My darling Sandy, I know you love Damian with your whole being but have you thought of the family's disagreement?" Hailey began.

"You heard his father. Would Damian stay happy in the marriage if things are not all right in his family?" Spencer asked.

"I think you should find a way to resolve the situation, for both your happiness," Bridget added.

Sandy nodded, and the girls left her to sit by themselves. She looked over at Damian who was dozing slightly. He looked so at peace, that she promised never to take away his peace.

"I have to step up my game. After we get back to New York, I will enroll at the Columbia Business School. I have to bring something to the table if I want to convince the Remington that I am worthy of their name," Sandy thought.

Oklahoma seemed different, just after some months she left. The biggest change was with her family. They wanted to please her at every turn and did not pick on her as they did before. Her mother kept asking her what she wanted to eat, even after five minutes of a meal. As for Damian, they worshiped the ground he walked on. He soon became a friend for all as he riddled them with stories of his travels to countries they had never dreamed of. Unknown to Sandy, her wedding was being organized.

Sandy woke up on Saturday morning and found a cloth bag and a note by her bedside. She smiled, thinking it was one of Damian's usual gifts. Excited to read what Damian had to say, she opened the note and stared wide-eyed at the four words written on it.

"Will you marry me?"

"Oh my God!" Sandy rushed to the door and flung it open, only to find her best friends dressed up for bridesmaid duties. "What is going on here?"

"You are getting married, baby girl." The girls got in and pushed her to the bathroom.

"We have to bring you to the church in exactly one hour. We don't want to keep the groom waiting, do we now?"

Sandy could not contain her excitement. She never imagined that Damian was planning their wedding. With his family's disapproval, she thought that it would be a while before they could get married. Now, she understood her family's new behavior; she was no longer Sandy whom nothing worked for, but Sandy who was getting married to a wealthy heir.

"Finally, I can build a home with the one I love," Sandy thought with tears cascading down her face. Now more than ever, she knew she had to step up and bring something to the table.

After her shower, her bridesmaids dressed her up in the white bejeweled wedding dress. It was made of silk, with an open boat neckline and a full skirt, heavy because of the precious stones sewn into it.

"This is the most beautiful wedding dress I ever saw!" Hailey was amazed by the elegance of the luxurious wedding dress.

Sandy looked beautiful, not because of the costly dress, or the silver tiara holding the five meters long veil, but because of her eyes. They danced with happiness and were illuminated with hope.

The bride and her entourage arrived at the Calvary church, where Sandy attended church with her family, before leaving Oklahoma., in a white, decorated limousine. They were however told by the church workers, to wait in the car, as the groom was yet to be seen.

"Why isn't Damian here?" Sandy asked no one in particular.

An angry Lucia, dressed in a white jumpsuit with a fur coat in the same color over it, alighted from the rented car in front of the Colcord hotel in Oklahoma. She walked briskly to the front desk and bestowed one of her icy glares on the poor young woman.

"I am Lucia Remington and thankfully, I own a sizable number of shares in this hotel. That is why you should think before you refuse my request," Lucia said.

"How can I help you, ma'am?" the young receptionist asked.

"I am looking for my son, Damian Remington. He is here, isn't he?" Lucia asked.

"It is against..." the young woman began, but Lucia cut her off.

"Remember to think carefully before rejecting my request," Lucia said.

"All right let me check." The tapped a few keys and looked at her computer screen. "He checked out just a few minutes ago. He is going to his wedding."

"Where?" Lucia asked, her eyes were no longer cool, but frightened.

"At the Calvary church..."

Before the young woman could complete her statement, Lucia hurried out of the lobby to the waiting car.

"Driver, please, do you know the Calvary church?" Lucia asked the moment she stepped into the car.

"Oh yes, it is not far from here," the driver replied.

"Step on the gas!"

As the driver navigated through traffic, Lucia kept her eyes out of the window, scanning every car and its occupants. She could not imagine what would happen if Damian married Sandy before she could stop him.

She was sitting in her study at the manor when Nicole barged in and told her there was a situation concerning Damian and Sandy.

"I know they went for a vacation in her hometown, but there is no cause for alarm. I am working on someone to sabotage her when she comes back from her trip," Lucia said.

"Then it would be too late because then, she would be Mrs. Remington," Nicole said coolly.

"What are you saying?" Lucia asked, standing up abruptly.

"It is not a vacation...Damian has planned a surprise wedding. I only found out now, because I put a tail on both."

Without wasting time, she had flown from New York to Oklahoma and with the help of the P.I Nicole hired, found the hotel Damian was staying in. Now she was here, but it seemed she had come too late.

Her blood pressure would have gone up, she thought, because her breathing had become uneven. For the first time in a long while, Lucia Remington was afraid. Then she surprised herself; she closed her eyes and said a prayer to God. The last time she prayed was when she still attended catechism before she married Carl.

"Stop!" Lucia commanded. They had driven past a car parked by the side of the road. A young man was standing by it and he looked exactly like her son.

Lucia stepped out of the car and walked backward, towards the parked car she saw. As she came nearer, she saw it was indeed Damian and from where she was, she could hear his conversation with the man who appeared to be his driver.

"I don't know if I am doing the right thing. I love Sandy, but I also love my family and our union will bring nothing but war," Damian said, rubbing his head the way he always did when he was confused. "I don't know if I am ready to sacrifice my family for the love of my life."

"Is it really about the unity of your family or are you afraid to lose the luxury?" the driver asked. "The cars, private jets, big houses, and the name. If your father disowns you, you are no longer a Remington, in name at the least."

"Forget that, are you ready to allow my enemy to win?" Lucia asked as she got to them.

"Mother? Why are you here?" Damian was amazed, so much that he looked at her like she was an apparition.

"You are just going to give the keys to the kingdom to the son of the woman who took your father's love away from your mother?" Lucia continued.

"What are you talking about, mother?" Damian asked.

"Your father has a mistress and a bastard." Lucia dropped the bombshell. "What the Remington dynasty is today, is because of my dynasty which I brought when I married your father. But now, he is just going to give it to a woman and her son, who know nothing about our family. They have no rights, but they want to reap and this shenanigan with Sandy is delivering the keys of the kingdom right into their hands."

"Mother, my father has a son that is not me?" Damian asked.

"Exactly! He is the same man who won the horse race at the ranch retreat, and your father made that happen. He is also registered at the club which is only for our family and friends. Slowly, he is bringing him into the family, because he has lost faith in you."

"Oh no," Damian said as he remembered all his father had said during the phone conversation and at the private airfield. Everything became clearer in his mind. His father was truly going to disinherit him because he had another heir.

Chapter Ten

The only thing Hector had from his father, Carl Remington, was his dark brown hair and his pointy chin. He was weathered, not like the blue blood finesse Carl Remington had. Hector grew up envying his friends, whose father brought them to soccer practice, right from when he was a little boy.

"Why does daddy never come home? Is he mad at us?" he had asked his mother.

"No, he just has a lot to do abroad. He loves you!" his mother said.

"But he never calls to check up on me. Does he not love me?"

"How can you say that, Hector? Your father loves you and one day you would know," his mother replied.

Was this the day, Hector wondered as he stared at his mother, sitting across him at the breakfast table. She had just told him that he was a Remington like it was the most normal thing for her to say. In the same breath, she told him his father wanted him to join the company.

"He sponsored you through the best schools for this reason, so you could one day take over from him," Jennifer, his mother said.

"Are you hearing yourself right now? The man has a son, a legitimate son, who is heir to the fortune," Hector replied, running his hand through his hair.

"Not if I have something to do with it...you are your father's son and you deserve all that belongs to you."

"Whatever..." Hector stood up and left the table.

"You have a meeting with your father this evening, so be home before seven," his mother called after him.

Hector took his car keys and left the house. He entered his car and drove to the 'Grill,' a restaurant that served different meat dishes. It was his restaurant which he founded, all on his own.

From when Hector was a teenager, he stopped waiting for his father to come home. He had read enough to know that he was an illegitimate child and his father probably had a family of his own. So, he began to rely on himself, even though they lived comfortably. He saved up every money he got and in senior year of high school, while other kids were excited about prom, he was building his first business. He had always loved food and so whenever his mother was in the kitchen, he stood there and watched. So, he learned how to make a pudgy sandwich, which he sold in school during recess. Even though his schoolmates laughed at him for being a sissy, they ditched the school cafeteria for his homemade pudgy sandwiches. Soon, he added chocolate toppings and increased the price. Every time he added something new, he increased the price. Then he started making lemonades, which he served with the sandwiches.

Through this business, Hector learned the ropes of doing business and of profit and loss, even though he had no father guiding him. His mother had one string after another of boyfriends and so she left him to his own devices. After high school, he got into UPenn, to study business administration. Straight out of college, he enrolled in Columbia Business School, for his MBA. Afterward, he launched his restaurant, which he always wanted to do.

"Now, I am fine. I never needed you, daddy and I don't need you now," Hector said as he drove his car into the parking lot of his glass wall restaurant.

While Hector was out, his mother, Jennifer called Carl and arranged a dinner meeting. When she dropped the call, she called her gym instructor to come over for a class. She also called the boutique she frequented and asked them to deliver a black evening dress to her residence. She wanted to look her best for Carl. For years, she had warmed his bed and looked good for him. Perhaps it had not gotten him to divorce his wife and marry her, but it had got him to finally put her son in the loop.

"From the way Damian is going, my son may well be the new heir of the Remington fortune," Jennifer thought, then she remembered Lucia's veiled threat.

"What can she possibly do?" Jennifer scoffed.

At the dinner, she would show Carl, that his son which he forsook for so long, was way better than the one in his house.

"I am proud of my son and all his achievements..." she let her voice trail off as she paced the living room. "Through him, I will get everything I want in this life."

Jennifer burst into laughter. "Go on and marry your sweetheart, my dear Damian Remington. You will only be paving the way for my son."

Sandy was becoming antsy from waiting for her groom. It had been over an hour and there was no show from Damian. She tried calling him, but his numbers were unavailable.

"Sister Sandy, perhaps it is time to let the guests go," said the Reverend who was supposed to officiate the ceremony.

"It has just been an hour, let's wait for a little. Perhaps he is stuck somewhere," Sandy replied, even when she knew that there was not any traffic congestion by that time of day.

"I knew it was too good to be true. Our Sandy ain't that lucky," said her mother. "You should have just stayed where you were, instead of coming here to cause me disgrace."

"Mama, Damian is coming!"

They waited another hour; by this time some of the guests had already left. Only those who wanted to see the end stayed behind.

Then Sandy's phone rang.

She looked at her friends with tears in her eyes. She did not know why, but immediately the phone rang, she just knew whoever was calling would not give her good news. Now, seeing it was Damian calling, she did not know what news to expect.

"Go ahead...whatever it is, it is going to be all right," Hailey said, and squeezed her hand reassuringly.

"Hello, Damian." Sandy waited for the bad news she knew would come.

"My love, I have gone back to New York. My mother came to Oklahoma. There was an emergency and it involves my family."

"Wow." The tears cascaded down Sandy's face. "Just wow."

"If it was not important, I would not come back to New York. I sent someone to get you and your girls, plane tickets back home. We will talk when you are here." Damian's voice was firm, but underneath it, Sandy could hear uncertainty.

Sandy hung up the call without saying a word. "We are going back to New York," she told her friends.

"Oh my God, what happened?" Bridget asked.

"I don't know, but what I know is that the wedding is off." Sandy pulled the tiara and flung it. Then she left the limousine, deciding to walk from the church home.

"What happened, where is she going?" Her mother asked the three ladies.

"The wedding is off," Hailey said curtly.

"I knew it! That good for nothing daughter of mine has humiliated us all."

While Sandy walked home, she pulled off her shoes and flung them away. She was angry, hurt, and confused. Did he get cold feet or was it a family emergency, she wondered.

"His mother never wanted us together, so I am not surprised she came to stop him!" Sandy clenched her fist in anger. She was angry at Damian, for not having a backbone.

But she would never let go of the relationship until he explained to her the reason he stood her up.

As soon as Damian touched down in New York, he went in search of his father. When he looked at his phone and saw that the time was past four in the evening, he knew his father would be at the exclusive golf club. Quickly he got home and changed into his sports clothes.

On his drive over, he thought of the woman he should have married and the decision he must make. He loved her truly and could not imagine a life without her in it. Still, he also could not imagine being disinherited by his father. He could not imagine losing the Remington name and the accompanying privileges.

"What do I do?" Damian looked ahead and all he saw was bleak. He wanted to turn back and run to his fiancé. He wanted to tell her he was sorry and marry her immediately. But before he thought about it, he knew he couldn't do it, so he plowed on because there was no other solution. "I got to do what I got to do."

At the golf club, his father watched him as he approached. He was glad that Damian had come back to his senses. Before now, Lucia had called to tell him that he changed his mind. He was relieved when he heard that, even though she told him accompanied by so many words.

"Father..." Damian started. He dropped is a golf bag and began to stretch. Even though he was succumbing to his father's will, he did not want to give away his power.

"Damian, how can I help you?" Carl asked as he got ready to throw a ball.

"I have called off my wedding with Sandy, to marry Nicole and move the family forward, just as you wanted," Damian said with a straight face.

"To say I am happy about it, would be an understatement. I am glad you came around. I knew you would." Carl swung his golf club at the ball, with a smile on his face.

"But I have a condition..." Damian said and got his father to turn abruptly.

"Conditions?"

Damian did not allow him to continue, because if he did, he might lose the upper hand. "I want Sandy given a top managerial position. It would be compensation for everything I have put her through."

"Top managerial position?" Carl looked incredulous.

"Sandy is smart. Most of the deals we won were won through her input. She has a degree in business administration. That is my only condition."

"All right, you get what you want. This calls for a celebration."

"We will meet at dinner," Damian said and left with his golf bag. He did not come to play golf anyway. He felt resentment towards his father, for forcing him to give up his one great love.

"Talking about dinner, I was supposed to have dinner with Jennifer and Hector," Carl thought and then brought out his phone.

"Hello, I cannot make dinner anymore. Raincheck?" he said into the phone. After a while, he dropped the call and picked up his golf club.

Carl decided that he would do right by his illegitimate son. He would do what he should have done a long time ago; bring him on to the board and give him shares to the company. The dynasty would be put in Damian's hand, but his other son would also benefit because he was after all a Remington.

"It is time to rewrite my will," Carl said, just before striking the ball with his club.

Chapter Eleven

Instead of the alarm clock, it was the shrill sound of her phone ringing that woke Sandy from sleep. She looked to her phone on the bedside table and saw it was Damian calling. Her heart skipped a beat and then began to beat rapidly. She did not know what to expect, but she took the call anyway.

"Honey, did I wake you? I am sorry about that. Are you coming into the office today?" Damian asked the moment she received the call.

"Yes, I will come." Sandy sounded as calm as she could.

"We need to talk. I also have a surprise for you. So be punctual," Damian said.

"What is the problem? You are trying to sound happy and excited, but I know you well enough now to know that you are hiding something away from me." Sandy whisked away from a stray teardrop.

"You are imagining things, baby and it is understandable, given what I have put you through. No matter what happens, know that I love you so much. I have never loved any woman the way I love you. See you later, babe." Damian hung up the call.

Sandy went into her bathroom and took a long, warm bath. She tried to trust in Damian, inside her she could feel it that everything was about to go wrong in her life. To match her perturbed feeling, she dressed up in a black fur dress and tied her hair up in silk, black scarf. She dabbed little powder on her face and she was ready to go. She had no will to look pretty because nothing was all right with her.

In all her thoughts, she stayed away from thinking about her mother and her siblings. If she did, she would end up crying.

In the elevator, her phone rang with Hailey's call. It made her remember what her friends told her on the flight to Oklahoma with Damian.

"Why didn't I think of this?" Sandy berated herself, as for the first time in many days, a smile broke on her face. "I can give Damian peace and the right room to love me if I can convince his family I am good for him."

Although Sandy knew what she should do, she did not know how to go about it. How in the world could she convince the Remington's that she, who had no name or pedigree, no inheritance or dynasty, was good enough for Damian, against a woman who had everything she did not have. The train ride from her side of town to Rem Energy Towers was filled with despair.

"Why can't you just let go before you get hurt?" an inner asked her.

"Why can't I?" Sandy asked. She thought back to her ex. She had loved him, even though it was not with as much intensity. He had not even done as much as standing her up at the altar and she left. But with Damian, it was different. Hailey always said a woman had two chances at love.

"The first time is your first love and a woman never forget her first love," Hailey would say. "But the second love she would have is her one great love. If she lost that love, she would never find love again."

Hailey always said it might take several heartbreaks and wrong men to find a woman's one great love, but when she did, it was always hard to let go.

"Perhaps, Damian is my one great love and if I lose him, I would never find love again. Perhaps, this is the reason I cannot let go." Sandy pondered these thoughts in her head, as she walked into the lobby of Rem Energy.

As if her morning was not bad enough, she walked right into Lucia Remington. The matriarch looked at her with disdain in her eyes. Then a mocking smile broke on her face.

"How does it feel to be dumped?" Lucia asked, sneering at her. "You thought you found your ladder to the top but see who has been brought down to her face."

"What are you talking about, ma'am?" Sandy asked. "Who has been dumped?"

"You, my darling. How does it feel being stood up at your wedding? If I were you, I would be too ashamed to show my face here again. But shame is alien to many people these days." Lucia sighed and shook her head in pity. "As for me, I am just happy you are out of my son's life."

Sandy could not take it anymore, so she walked out on Lucia. "She is just taunting me....it isn't possible that Damian has yielded to them and sacrificed our happiness."

When Sandy got to her office which was led into Damian's office, she was surprised to find that her things had been packed into a box. Her heart began to beat faster as she remembered what Lucia Remington had told her just a few minutes ago.

"No, it's not true." Sandy gasped.

"Yes, it's true," Damian said as he walked out of his office with a smile on his face.

"What is going on, Damian?" Sandy asked.

"I don't need you here anymore, but the company needs you more. Therefore I suggested that you become the head of the product analysis department and the board agreed."

"What?" Sandy did not look thrilled by the news. "With a business degree. I don't even have an MBA!"

"I did help, but I wouldn't have if I didn't believe you could do it. You are smart and a fast learner, babe."

"I don't know, it just seems sudden and out of place. Damian, what is going on?" Sandy dropped her tote bag and pulled out a chair. "First you stand me up at the altar and now this. I just met your mother in the lobby and she seems to think our relationship is over. She asked me how it feels to be dumped."

Damian sighed heavily and pulled a chair too. He sat and looked at Sandy. His lips smiled, but his eyes were sad. "I love you Sandy, but my family will disinherit me if I get married to you."

"Oh great!" Tears gathered fast in Sandy's eyes as her voice began to shake. "This new position is to compensate me, right?"

"In my father's eyes, yes. But for me, this is me allowing you to prove to my family that you bring something to the table too."

Damian stood up and began to pace. "I can't let you go. I love you that much and I would die first before I let go of a loyal woman. I agreed to my family to get them off your back. You saw what happened at the annual retreat, and that is just the tip of the iceberg." Damian thought of the sex tape that would have been aired if he had not stopped it. His mother would go to any length to get Sandy out of the way and he could not tolerate anyone making life difficult for her, not after what he was going to do to her.

"I lied to my family to buy time, to either convince them that Nicole is wrong for me or that you are right for me. So, you must play this charade with me, because I won't let you leave."

Sandy walked up to him and threw herself into his arms. She kissed him as tears of relief cascaded down her cheeks.

"I won't leave, baby." Sandy deepened the kiss, as her hormones took over. She pushed Damian against the wall and began to rip off his clothes.

Damian allowed his hands to run over her body, even as the guilt took over him. He missed her, and he wondered how he could let all they had to go. Perhaps I can have it both ways, he thought. He removed her clothes in a flurry of movements and then trailed kisses down her neck to the exposed mound of flesh. When his mouth covered her nipples, he heard her gasp with pleasure and it only fueled his passion. Before long, he had Sandy hanging on the wall, with her legs strapped around him, as they were locked in steaming lovemaking.

"I love you, Sandy, don't ever leave me." Damian thrust into her with all the pent-up passion in him.

"I won't ever leave you. I got your back," Sandy replied in between moans.

From Sandy's almost-empty office, they went to Damian's office and made love again on the couch and the floor covered with a Persian rug. Through it all, they promised to stay with each other and never leave.

"I have to find a way to destabilize the Walton businesses. If I can make Nicole worthless to my family, this marriage will be called off," Damian thought as he emptied the last drop of his life-giving force into Sandy.

With Sandy's permission, Damian engaged Nicole in a lavish engagement party. Sandy hid in her apartment as the reporters camped outside waiting for a sneak peek into what her life was after being stood up at the altar and having Damian engage another woman. There was a media onslaught on her, as some reporters called her a gold digger who never got to see a payday. She knew that most of these media reports were orchestrated and sponsored by Lucia Remington.

The girl's gang did not understand what was happening with their friend, Sandy. On the news, Damian was loving up on Nicole, with an engagement that was not half as costly as the one he gave Sandy. However, despite what they were seeing on the news, they had seen Damian sneaking out of Sandy's apartment many times.

"Are you so in love that you agreed to a mistress position?" Bridget asked when they gathered in Sandy's apartment for a sleepover, which they intended to be an intervention.

"What is wrong with that? Hailey dates married men, but Damian is not even married yet," Sandy replied.

"Oh girl, don't even go there. I date these men for fun, not with my heart. I see how much you love this man and I don't understand how you can tolerate being the side piece."

"You don't know what you are saying, I am the real piece and what you think you are seeing, is just a facade." Sandy left her friends in the bedroom and went to her living room.

She trusted Damian, but she also needed to do something on her own. How could she convince the Remington's that she was worthy, she asked herself for the umpteenth time?

"I should create a great product idea..." she thought.

Unfortunately for the love birds, it was not only Sandy's friends who noticed that they were still having a secret relationship, despite Damian's engagement to Nicole. Lucia had felt something was not right, especially as Sandy still worked at Rem Energy. For the few months her son had dated her, she had studied Sandy and knew she was like most poor people. Poor people had nothing to their name, save for their dignity and self-respect. Sandy was exactly that way and for her dignity, she would have quit from the company if Damian had ended the relationship. She knew something was wrong when Sandy was promoted to head a department, which her qualifications were not enough for. So, she commissioned a private investigator to watch Sandy and Damian. Within a few days, she had found the truth; her son was still seeing Sandy.

"But why?" she had asked herself. She did not know the game they were playing until the Walton's had dinner with the Remington's.

That evening, the families were seated at the table, with Nicole beaming with smiles. Damian asked a lot of questions about the Walton business and even suggested that before the wedding, he is admitted into the board of directors.

"This would send a message of a united front, besides both businesses are going to be joined anyways," Damian had said.

Lucia had wondered why Damian was interested in merging the companies, especially as this had never been discussed with his father. Then it dawned on her that her son was not interested in merging the companies. If he was, he would have asked that it was done, instead of admitting him on the board of directors.

"He said that as bait, so they could allow him on the board. For him to be on the board, he would need shares at the company. Why?" Lucia pondered throughout dinner.

She realized that her son was an expert at hostile takeovers; he had helped the family acquire competitors that way and he was hoping to do the same to the Walton company. He could only want to do this without his father's instructions if he wanted to render Nicole worthless.

"Smart idea...the only problem is I know now what you want to do," Lucia thought and so she made a counter plan.

"Even after standing her up at the altar and all the media onslaught on her, she still holds on to my son. My son is not that steadfast, so perhaps I should give him a reason to leave," Lucia thought with a sly smile on her face, which the other diners did not notice because they were engrossed with what Damian was proposing.

"You won't know what hit you, Sandy, until it is done with you." Lucia chuckled.

"Lucia darling is there something amusing?" Carl asked, giving her a hard look, even though he was smiling.

"Oh, nothing at all," Lucia replied.

Lucia was also too engrossed in hatching her plans against Sandy, that she did not notice the nervousness of Nicole's parents. They had something to hide, but she did not see it.

The family was gathered at the breakfast table when Carl announced that he had invited someone for breakfast.

"I invited this person over here because I have an announcement to make," Carl said.

Mother and son turned to look at each other, wondering if it was what they were thinking it was. The butler came and interrupted them as he whispered in Carl's ears.

"The young man has arrived. Should I send him in?" the butler whispered, even though it was audible enough for the others at the table to hear.

"Of course, send him in immediately," Carl said.

After a few minutes, the handsome, brown-haired Hector walked in. It was so obvious that they would look stupid if they pretended they did not know.

"Father, you have another son?" Damian asked, even though he already knew the truth.

"Yes, Damian. He is your brother and I want him to be part of the family." Carl beckoned on Hector to take a seat at the table.

"I will not allow him to stay in this house, do you understand what I am saying?"

"I don't want to stay in this house. I told you that before," Hector turned to Look at Carl. "I am here because of my mother."

"Of course, the tramp is tired of spreading her legs for money and has resorted to using her son," Lucia said bitingly.

"I will not sit here and listen to my mother being called names." Hector stood from the seat and made to leave.

"You don't have to leave. Let's speak in the study." Carl left the table and beckoned on Hector to follow him.

"She is seeing her again, that is why he has suddenly remembered his father's duties to her bastard." Lucia fumed and could no longer eat her food. "I have lost my appetite."

When his mother left, Damian picked at his food, while he thought of the whole scenario. Even if he destabilized Walton's business, his father would expect him to land another good bride with million-dollar assets. His father was that greedy, or maybe he was not, Damian thought. After all, every businessman needed a network; it was better if your network was linked by family ties. After seeing Hector, Damian did not doubt in his mind that his father would not hesitate to make Hector his heir. There was no denying that he was likable and had the grit; something his father said was the traits of a successful entrepreneur. Something he did not have.

"Do you want to destabilize the Walton business? Nicole is the only chip you have, that your stepbrother does not," an inner voice said to him.

Chapter Twelve

Sandy walked into the exclusive country club run by the Remington family, where she had just become a member, with Damian's influence. She came there to stay away from distractions because she was working on a new product for Rem Energy. After sitting at the secluded bar, she went to work on her laptop. She was barely through the first page of her proposal when a shadow fell upon the front of her table.

"I don't want anything, except quietness," Sandy said thinking it was the barman. She had chosen the bar because it was the only part of the club that was empty at that time of day.

"I have not offered anything yet," the voice said.

When Sandy looked up, she saw a tall, dark-skinned man, sporting a Mohawk haircut and a cocky smile. "Oh, you are not the barman, silly me," Sandy said, taking a glance at the well-tailored suit and the air around him.

"Yes, can I join you?' the man asked.

"I don't want company because I am working on something really important..." Sandy was saying.

"Oh sorry, I will just go." The man started to leave, but Sandy stopped him.

Sandy felt she was being rude unnecessarily and so she called him back. "Come on, you can share the table."

"I am Mitch and it is my pleasure to be meeting such a fine lady," the man said.

"Sandy here," Sandy said with a small smile.

Soon, the proposal before her was completely forgotten, as she talked with the stranger on several different topics important to her. They argued and learned from each other, so much that it felt like he had known her for a long time. Sandy only noticed how far the time was spent when the early bar strollers walked in. She looked out and saw that the sun was already going home.

"Oh my, the time is far spent. I ended up not doing what brought me here," Sandy said without any forms of regret.

"What are you working on?" Mitch asked.

"Oh, just a new product I want my company to launch," Sandy replied.

"Oh, you work at Rem Energy. Now I see. I was trying to decide how you are a member of this club because you don't look like the rich dolls."

"What?" Sandy feigned surprise. "Are you saying I look poor?"

"No, you are more down to earth than the rich trust fund dolls around here."

"I understand." Sandy understood what he was saying, even before he explained. She had never felt such affinity with someone, except with Damian.

"Damian! Oh, I have plans. I must leave now." Sandy began to gather her things into the bag.

"Damian? Could that be Damian Remington?" Mitch asked.

Sandy was taken aback because she could not allow anyone to know she was still seeing Damian. "Oh yeah, I am to submit another proposal to him before the day ended. I will just rush over to Rem Energy."

"Not before giving me a number, I can reach you at." Mitch held her hand.

Sandy blushed and then she gave him his card. Since falling in love with Damian, she had never felt attracted to any man. This was the first time she was affected by a man's touch; a man that was not Damian.

A few weeks later, Sandy pitched the product to the board of directors. While Damian felt proud, Carl was impressed and surprised at Sandy's intelligence. As for Lucia, she smiled all through the presentation, because Sandy was playing right into her hands.

"Surprisingly, it is a good idea that would boost our revenue base. I did not expect it from such a person," Lucia said and made sure her disgust showed on her face. "But we need to get on board with this, regardless."

"I do not agree with all my mother has said, but I think she is right about the ingenuity of the product idea."

"However, the best thing would be to partner with another company in the energy sector to take the burden of the cost of this project. Do you have such?" Carl asked.

"That wouldn't be an issue, sir," Sandy said, remembering the many clients she and Damian had worked with, before this time.

"Then it is settled. The appropriate department will approve and then you can draw up a time-line," Carl said and left the board room.

Sandy tried approaching some of the companies they had worked with before, but unfortunately, the fact that she was no longer a Remington favorite, reduced her clout with these companies.

"I don't know what to do. You know why I am doing this, right?" Sandy asked while she lay on Damian's chest, after a bout of steamy sex, in a secluded resort in Hampton.

"I know, but I trust you can figure it out on your own. Why don't you look away from these big companies and try the smaller companies? They would jump at the offer and then it would be up to you to choose," Damian replied.

"Wow, that's an idea. What would I do without you?"

So, Sandy implemented Damian's idea and sent out notices to smaller energy companies, to work with her on a new product. She got many replies and had to narrow down to a few reputable companies.

The next day, she was in her office going over the scheme of the product when she heard footfalls. There was a knock and Mitch walked in, looking dapper in his customary power suit. Since the day at the club bar, they had only exchanged a few phone calls.

"What a surprise... how can I help you?" Sandy asked, as she stood up and walked over to Mitch.

"I am here representing my company...Gold-leaf Energy," Mitch replied with a smile.

"Oh, all right...let's get right into it." They went over a few bases and then got into the thick of things, where they discussed milestones and product completion.

Sandy found herself amazed at Mitch's intelligence, especially his ability to know what she needed for the product to be a success. After Mitch, there were other company representatives and they also came with a good game, but Sandy knew she wanted to work with Mitch. Therefore, at the end of the day, it was Mitch she called to tell him they would be working together. After the call, she packed her bags and left the company building. She did not want to go home just yet because the house would be so lonely, seeing as Damian could not come over that night. So, she drove her new silver Mercedes Benz to a Karaoke bar and was oblivious of the tail behind her.

Sandy got herself a glass of cherry and nursed it while she listened to love songs. "If love was so sweet, then why was it so hard for her to enjoy her love with Damian?" she pondered this.

"A penny for your thoughts?" a voice broke into her thoughts. She turned and saw Mitch looking down at her with a smile on his sexy face. He was not wearing a power suit, but a dress pant and a cashmere top; he looked relaxed and oh so sexy.

"Gather your thoughts, Sandy. He is not as sexy as my Damian," Sandy thought as she smiled absentminded at him.

"Come on, you did not come to the bar to drink Cherry, did you?" Mitch chuckled, looking into her glass.

"I came for the music, you know."

"Then I am going to sing you a song." Mitch walked over to the front of the bar and took the microphone.

"I wrote this song, but never found someone I could sing it to. But tonight, I want to sing this song to my beautiful Sandy," he said looking straight at her.

There was applause as he began to sing. He sang as though it was from his heart and soon the bar was applauding him. Then he went over to where Sandy was and pulled her up.

"Mitch, what are you doing?" Sandy asked.

"Relax my lady. I will never hurt you," Mitch replied in a calm voice while looking deep into Sandy's eyes.

He took her to the front and then he began to sing a fast song while spinning Sandy around. Sandy got into the spirit and began to move her hips to the song. Soon, the other people in the bar joined them in dancing. Sandy was having so much fun that she forgot all about her gloominess.

The night was far spent when they both came out of the bar. They walked hand in hand to her car. But before Sandy could enter her car, Mitch held her hand back and turned her to face him.

"A woman knows when a man likes her. So, I guess you are pretending like you don't." Mitch came too close to her, that Sandy was suddenly unable to breathe.

"Mitch...I am engaged..." Sandy stuttered.

"Engaged to Damian Remington?" Mitch asked. "We both know he is getting married to Nicole Walton. It is time for you to get out before you find yourself stranded. I genuinely like you."

"I am sorry, I am not available." Sandy entered her car and drove off.

The next day, Sandy entered her office and met a big bouquet. She took out the note and saw it was from Mitch. He apologized for coming on too strong and hoped they could work together and remain friends. Sandy was still smiling at the gold embossed paper when Damian walked in. He rushed to her and kissed her.

"I missed you so much," Damian said. Then he saw the flowers; Sandy hid the note behind her. "Who gave you flowers?"

"Oh, it is from Gold-leaf Energy. You know we have been working together on the new product..." Sandy found herself blabbing.

Sandy did not know why she lied. The flowers were not from Gold-leaf Energy, but from Mitch and it was for a personal reason, not a business.

"I have to end this so-called friendship before it gets out of hand," Sandy thought.

If only she knew what it would cost her, she would have ended it long ago.

Later that day, Mitch came over, so they could put finishing touches on product formulation before it went into production. They worked until the sun went home and then it began to get dark. However, they were able to finish.

"We did it!" Sandy was so happy. This meant a lot to her because she was closer to proving herself to the Remington family.

"We deserve a hot dinner and I know a great place we can have it," Mitch said.

"I should..." Sandy started.

"No, don't reject me. Friends don't reject offers from one another. I have something I want to discuss with you."

"All right, all right."

From the office, Mitch drove her to a restaurant in Brooklyn Heights where they had dinner and talked about life.

"Why don't you get an MBA? I understand not getting it before, because you could not afford it. But now, you can do that, it would be wise to invest in your future.," Mitch said.

"It has been on my mind recently. But I was going to get it after my wedding to..." Sandy stopped herself before she spilled the secret between her and Damian.

After dinner, Mitch drove her back home amid talks and laughter in the car. It was a good friendship that would have been beneficial if it was genuine.

When Mitch got to her apartment, he rushed out to open the door for her. Sandy giggled, as she enjoyed the treatment and the respect Mitch was giving her.

"Thanks, Mitch, for dinner," Sandy said and turned to go, but Mitch took her hand and turned her to face him.

It was so sudden that Sandy stumbled and fell forward, with her hands splayed on his chest. Mitch took the moment without hesitation and brought down his lips on hers. Sandy was so shocked that she stood still, while Mitch forced her lips apart and deepened the kiss. It was only when Sandy regained control of herself, that she pushed Mitch away and gave him a hard slap across the face.

"What do you think you are doing?" Sandy asked.

"Why are you denying the fact that you feel something for me?"

"Don't delude yourself, my heart has only one occupant and it is Damian." Sandy walked away and ran into the lobby of the apartment building she lived in.

Her back was turned, and she never looked back, or else she would have seen the cocky smile on Mitch's face.

Chapter Thirteen

⸺⸱⟨⟩⸱⸺

T ime was running out and yet, Damian had not found any way to render Nicole worthless to his family. He was tired of the charade because he missed the love of his life, Sandy. So, he took out his phone to call Sandy, so they could plan a secret getaway, but the door to his office opened and an angry Nicole walked in.

"Wow, why the face on you?" Damian asked, putting the phone down.

"I don't get how you get to choose a slutty bitch, who just wants to climb up the social ladder, over a loyal woman like me. I see what you have been doing, dragging your feet to pick a wedding date, putting me and my family under stress," Nicole said.

"What is all this about?" Damian asked, with confusion etched on his face.

Nicole flung a magazine at him. "Take that, that is the woman you hurt me and keep hurting me for."

Splayed on the cover page was Sandy and Mitch locked in a kiss, with the title 'Damian's Ex-Fiancée finds love again.'

He flipped open to the page where the story was and found more pictures of Sandy and Mitch at the restaurant, the Karaoke bar dancing and in the parking lot, locked in an embrace. Sandy always looked happy and it irked Damian.

"She has a lover and has been leading on...egging me to find a way for us to be together," Damian thought as his hands clenched over the magazine.

"Pick a date for the wedding," Damian said.

"Next week...I will make the arrangements," Nicole replied, trying to hide her excitement.

Damian opened his checkbook and signed off some money for the wedding preparations. As he did this, he remembered how he was going to leave all the luxury behind for the love of Sandy.

"I was even ready to destabilize my company shares, just to prove a point...all for a disloyal woman," Damian thought with anger.

"Thank you for seeing the truth," Nicole said before walking away.

It was a dinner party thrown for the Remington company investors and a party to launch the new product. Sandy was dressed gorgeously in a white lace dress that was just below her knee. The dress was trimmed with gold and accentuated her brown gold tone. Her hair was in curly waves down her back, just the way Damian liked it. Throughout the day before, she has been unable to reach out to Damian, because she had been busy at the plant. Therefore, she could not know that Damian had ended their relationship and chose a date for his wedding with Nicole. She searched for him at the party but could not find him.

In her search for Damian, she walked out into the dimly lit garden. Then she began to hear Nicole's voice and slowly she walked towards that direction, wondering why Nicole was here when Damian was not.

"The bank was going to foreclose on the house and our company, we had to come up with this plan or else, we would have been disgraced. My daddy made bad decisions and plunged the Walton company into so much debt that we lost everything repaying some of the debts."

"What?" Sandy was beyond shocked. "She has nothing to her name and the Remington's are ready to force her on their son?"

Sandy knew she had just been given a weapon to get her fiancé back, with the support of his family, but she needed proof. And she knew where to look for one.

Sandy left the party immediately and went back to her apartment. She opened her laptop and began to search for financial databases, like Lexis, to get the EDGAR filings for the Walton company. She requested to access the file, as she posed as a member of the Remington family. She was told it would be sent to her email, after approval. Excited about this development, Sandy wanted to share the news, so she called Damian. After several rings, there was the dial tone, because Damian did not pick up.

"What is going on?" Sandy wondered.

The next day, the report was sent to her as promised and she quickly printed it out. She would go to the manor and tell everyone what she had overheard. The report in her hand would back up her story. On her way out, she ran into her girl's gang, as they were coming to her.

"Sandy, we are so sorry," Hailey said and hugged her.

"I don't know why you are saying sorry, but I can't ask you, because I am on my way to somewhere important," Sandy replied and rushed out into the parking lot.

"Where is she going in such a hurry?" Bridget asked.

"We should go after her. I hope she is not trying to hurt herself," Spencer said and then whisked a drop of tear from her eyes.

"It is so unfair. Men are scum." Hailey walked away, stomping her feet as she went, and her friends went after her.

On the drive to the Remington manor, Sandy could not contain her excitement. "Finally, they would see who the better woman is; a woman with potential or a woman evil enough to conceal such detail about her family." When she got to the manor, she was allowed in with the help of her staff ID. But when Sandy entered, she saw that it was decorated as though a ceremony would take place there. Then there was music and more people she had seen at the manor.

"Oh no, did Damian plan a surprise wedding again?" Sandy smiled as she drove up to the house.

"Ma'am, the ceremony is in the garden." The security man waved her towards the garden.

"I am looking for Mr. Remington senior and his wife," Sandy said.

"They are at the ceremony. It is a happy day for them." The security man all smiled.

Sandy did not think it was a surprise wedding for her anymore, so she parked her car and walked to the garden, with brisk footsteps. She did not know why her heart suddenly felt cold and her palms sweaty. When she got to the garden, her eyes met with Lucia Remington, who first had surprise on her face, then a wicked grin. Then Sandy's eyes went to the couple standing with a priest.

"By the powers vested in me, I pronounce you husband and wife," the priest said. "You may or may not kiss the bride. It is your choice."

The guests burst into laughter and then the noise of appreciation as Damian held Nicole and kissed her.

"Damian!" Sandy cried a guttural cry, which drew the attention of the guests.

Everyone turned and saw Sandy standing there with a piece of paper in hand. Damian looked at her and did not understand why she looked so broken. Was she not cheating on him with a man named Mitch, he wondered. Before he could decide on what to do, Sandy turned and ran away.

When Sandy took to her heels, she did not know where she was going, neither did she see where she was going. All she wanted to do, was get away as far as she could. Then it slammed into her, with such force that forced her out of the agony she felt. She felt the pain, but she saw the big G wagon.

"Oh...I hope I don't survive this," Sandy thought as she fell to the ground. Blood began to ooze out of her mouth. It hurt so badly, and the darkness called to her.

"There is nothing left here anymore. No one loves me...not my family and not even the man I have loved more than life itself," Sandy thought as the darkness slowly slipped in and overtook her.

"Sandy!" Damian ran towards the woman sprawled on the ground.

He got to her and knelt to take her head in his arms. He did not mind that the blood had stained his white tuxedo. All he cared for was the woman in his arms, whose eyes were tightly shut with blood oozing from her mouth. She looked like a broken doll.

"Oh my God, she rushed into my path like lightening. Oh no," Hector said as he rushed out of his car and went to Sandy.

"You hit her!" Damian was angry.

Hector called the ambulance and when they came, he went into the truck with them.

"I am coming with you," Damian said.

"You are going nowhere. You are married now, and I will not allow you prance around town with that ratchet girl." Nicole held his arm and pulled him away.

"Brother, you do not need to come. I got it covered," Hector said before the ambulance drove away.

Chapter Fourteen

Nicole took a walk around the manor, to relive her victory over Sandy. She went to the garden and inhaled the fresh smell of chrysanthemum.

"I am now a member of this wealthy family and by God, I will make the Walton's great again," Nicole thought as a satisfied smile slowly burst on her face.

As she was walking out of the garden, she found a piece of paper on the floor. It looked out of place, especially as she remembered it was the spot where Sandy had been hit by a car. She bent and picked up the paper, only for her eyes to bulge out in shock, when she read what the paper held.

"What! Who had this?" Nicole was shocked as her heart began to race faster.

"What are you going to do now? Shred-it and find out who knows?" a voice said behind her.

She turned and saw Lucia Remington; whose eyes were rock hair and blazing with fury.

"What...what are you talking about?" Nicole asked with a nervous smile.

"You know what I am talking about. How dare you deceive me?" Lucia grabbed her arm and dug her fingers into her flesh.

"I...I..."

"What are you going to say? I was stupid to have trusted you, you gold-digging bitch." Lucia flung her away.

Nicole knew she had been found out, but she couldn't cower before Lucia, or so she thought.

"And what if I lied about the true state of things, I have more pedigree than that Sandy of a girl would ever have." Nicole began to walk away.

"I will not tell anyone about this, for the sake of my son, but you will regret the day you made me an enemy. I have already started, I advise you to call your parents." It was Lucia's turn to walk away.

Nicole took her phone and dialed her father's number. The moment she picked, she heard wailing in the background.

"Father, what is going on?" Nicole could not keep the panic out of her voice.

"You should ask your mother-in-law. She made the bank foreclose early and has bought the mansion. She is in the process of taking over our company at a peanut price. We are finished, and it is all your fault." Her father hung up the call.

"What have I gotten myself into? I left someone I loved, to marry Damian, for the sake of family, yet, nothing has gone right," Nicole thought to herself as she paced up and down. Tears filled her eyes as she thought of all she had lost; it was not even about her family's dwindling assets, but the love she lost.

When she initiated the break up between her and Damian years ago, she knew that there was someone out there for her, but she did not know that it would be a man of lesser status. She met Colby and she just knew that they were made for each other. They met at the bar he owned downtown. That day she stayed in the office until late and in a bid to relieve stress, she drove downtown. She was attracted by the crowd at the front of the bar and went in to check. Despite the crowd, their eyes found one another. He was dark-skinned, macho looking, but with a beautiful smile that made him the kind of man that could protect you and still be tender with you.

"Hi, you are new here and..." Colby took a good look at her well-tailored pantsuit and her Zara bag, "you don't look like you belong to this crowd."

"I can belong wherever I want to," Nicole replied to him.

"Let me fix you a nice drink...on the house," Colby said, winking at her.

"Oh, when do barmen have such authority?"

"Oh sweetie, you don't know the half of it."

They both laughed, and she sat at the counter waiting for him to fix her a drink. While he did, they talked about several things including business in the city. She was surprised by his knowledge of tax and finance.

"Hey Mark, take over here," he removed his apron. "Come on, my lady."

He got them a table at the quieter side of the bar and cooked up a storm. When Nicole saw the plate of fried shrimps, salad dressing, and onion rings, her stomach began to rumble.

"I did not realize I was this hungry," Nicole said.

"A man who doesn't know when his woman is hungry does not deserve her," Colby replied.

The chemistry between them was so strong that when he tried to kiss her at the front of the bar, she did not refuse him. A kiss turned deep, and it took all of her to break away. That night, they both knew that it would not be the last time they saw.

But when her family went into financial crisis, Nicole knew she could not allow love to decide her choice of husband and so, when Lucia Remington approached her about marrying Damian, she did not think twice. She thought it was the salvation for their family, but now, it was their curse.

"I wonder how Colby is doing," Nicole thought.

As though her thoughts had conjured him, her phone started to ring. She looked at the number on her screen and could not believe Colby was calling her after so many months.

"Colby...Colby..." she said when she received the call.

"So, you went back to your ex and even married him. So, it was not that you weren't feeling the relationship anymore, but I was not your type of husband?" Colby's voice was calm, but underneath that calmness, Nicole could hear the anger.

"Colby, can I see you? I need you to understand why I did it." Nicole could not hold it anymore. It was as if hearing Colby's voice broke up the floodgates because she began to cry.

"No, princess. Please don't cry. I am sorry if I made you cry," Colby said.

"You did not make me cry...you have never made me cry. I am crying because I have made the worst mistake of my life."

"Can you come to the bar?" Colby asked.

"Yes," Nicole replied.

Nicole found that the bar had changed during the months she was apart from Colby. Before, it had been a bungalow and a homey bar, but now it was one story and had been given a makeover. When she saw Colby, she knew she had not come to talk, because she hugged him, pressing her body against his.

"I want you, Colby. That is all I need right now," Nicole said.

He took her through the back to his car outside and they drove to his new apartment. Colby did not think twice before claiming back his woman.

It was the first time she cheated on Damian, and it would not be the last.

Hector stayed by Sandy's bedside for all the time she was unconscious, until she finally opened her eyes. He watched her stare at him like he was a ghost. He tried to reassure her with a smile, but still, she looked scared.

"What happened to me and who are you?" Sandy asked with a hoarse voice.

"I am the unfortunate man who ran you over with a car. It was a mistake though. You ran right into me," Hector replied.

Sandy frowned as though she was trying to recollect. Then Hector watched as the memories came rushing back; all her painful memories of seeing Damian marry another woman, after promising her he would never leave her. She began to sob. It was painful to watch.

"It might seem painful now, but it dulls with time. Trust me." Hector went closer to her and pulled a chair.

"You don't know what you are saying. He was my great love and he just betrayed me without thinking twice." Sandy's voice was filled with anger and pain.

"He had no backbone...he did it all for the inheritance. Damn trust fund boy could not live without the big house, the fast cars, and all the luxurious vacation. He couldn't leave all that behind... not even at the feet of love." Sandy clenched and unclenched her fist repeatedly.

"I should call the doctor," Hector said and went out to call the doctor.

The doctor came back with Hector and began to examine Sandy.

"Take me away from here," Sandy said, fixing her eyes on Hector.

"You are not leaving yet until we say so. We need to carry out several tests to be sure there is no internal bleeding," the doctor said.

Sandy grimaced. Why wouldn't they let her go, she thought. She craved the solitude of her apartment because it would be the right place for her to take her life.

"I am the unluckiest person in this world. Why didn't I just die in the accident?" Sandy thought as fresh tears streamed down her eyes.

"Don't cry...it's going to be all right." Hector felt protective towards her and did not hold himself back from wiping her tears.

"It is never going to be all right, at least for me." Sandy turned her face to the wall and began to plan how she would take her life.

While Sandy was in the hospital, it was found that Gold-leaf Energy was a dummy company and the money REM Energy put into the new product had disappeared into thin air. It became worse when the pictures of Sandy and Mitch surfaced online.

"You were ready to abandon the family for her, but here she was, frolicking with another man who duped her," Carl said in anger.

"She probably was in collusion with the man," Lucia added.

"Sandy cared about the project. She could not have been in collusion with the man." Damian tried to defend Sandy.

"Really? She was sleeping with a man she did not know. You expect us to believe that?" Lucia asked.

"I am going to get the cops on her and make sure I recover all the company's funds," Carl walked away slamming the door after him.

"I know you wouldn't want her to go to prison, because as disloyal as she was, you loved her. I will help talk to your father to just fire her and let her go, but you have to promise to stay away from her for good," Lucia proposed to her son.

"I will," Damian said clenching his fist. "But not until I have had my answers."

Hailey, Bridget, and Spencer were at the hospital with Sandy, when Damian came. It was Hector, who told them about their friend's condition, as per Sandy's instruction. They blamed Damian for everything that happened to Sandy and when they saw him, they did not wait before attacking him.

"You have some nerve showing up here, you scum!" Hailey sneered at him.

"Haven't you done enough already?"

"There was nothing I did that was as bad as what Sandy did!" Damian pushed Hailey aside and went to Sandy, who stared at him with tears in her eyes. "How could you? You colluded with your lover to defraud my company?"

"What are you talking about?" Sandy managed in a low voice.

"Gold-leaf Energy is a dummy company and our funds for the product have disappeared into thin air. Here..." he shoved the magazine in her face.

Sandy's eyes widened when she saw all the pictures taken of her and Mitch. "Who did this?"

Hailey took the magazine and looked at it. Then she looked up at Sandy with surprise.

"It's not what you think. Mitch was my friend, or I thought he was. I never cheated on him. He is the one who betrayed me by marrying Nicole behind my back, but I am the one defending myself?"

"I only married Nicole because I found these and now, even after knowing you betrayed me, I am still protecting you from my father," Damian said. "I never thought there would be a day I would regret going to that bar where we met. But I never want to see you again."

"Go, you were never going to stay anyway. You are not a real man. You cannot stand without your family's wealth's Just leave and never come back," Sandy cried.

Damian shook his head and left.

"You three can leave as well. Leave!" Sandy screamed at the top of her voice.

"We will leave now, but know that, we will never leave your life. We are here for the good and the bad and we love you," Bridget replied.

"Come on girls, let's allow her rest. When I come back, you better be in a better mood," Hailey said, before leaving with the girls.

"My mother was right...I am so unlucky. Nothing has ever worked for me. I thought New York was the place my life would change for the better, but I was wrong." Sandy said to the empty room. "I can't do this anymore." Sandy stood up and removed all the IV sets connected to her. Then she walked out of her room, slowly because she felt pain in her stomach.

"Nurse, please how do I go up?" she asked a nurse she found in the hospital's corridor.

"Just use the elevator by the end of this hall, or take the stairs adjacent to it," the nurse explained.

"Thank you." Sandy walked away.

Hector drove into the hospital parking lot, locked his car, and began to walk to the front of the building. He wondered why he felt responsible for Sandy. Perhaps it was because he was the one who caused her accident, he thought. But deep within him, he knew he had never felt protective about anybody, except his mother. He was still deep in thoughts when he got to the front of the hospital and found people gathered there. They were looking upward, and Hector followed their gaze.

"Fuck!" Hector could not believe his eyes.

Sandy was standing at the edge of the roof, ready to throw herself about six stories down.

"Sandy!" Hector called, but of course Sandy did not hear.

Hector rushed into the lobby of the hospital and asked the receptionist how to get to the top floor. When he saw the elevator was taking time to come down, he ran to the stairs and began to take the stairs one after the other. As he ran up the stairs, he prayed that she was still standing there.

When he got to the top, he saw her make a move, and then he ran to her. "Sandy!" He grabbed her and pulled her to himself.

"What were you going to do?" He asked her.

"Who are you and why are you always there? I have nothing to do with you. So, leave me alone." Sandy struggled against him.

"I might not mean anything to you, but no man deserves you throwing away your life for him," Hector replied.

By this time, reporters had joined them at the terrace and were taking pictures of them.

"Get away and leave her alone," Hector shouted at them, as he used his hand to block Sandy's face.

He succeeded in taking Sandy down the stairs to the sixth floor where they took the elevator.

"I just want to end this meaningless life. I can't take it anymore," Sandy cried.

Hector said nothing but allowed her to cry. When he was younger and battling with his father's rejection, he learned that crying was therapeutic and healed the soul. So, he allowed her to cry.

In another part of the city, Carl and his wife was watching the drama of Sandy's attempted suicide. It baffled Carl, that his other son had also gotten entangled with Sandy.

"She just wouldn't leave this family alone!" Carl felt frustrated.

"Your bastard must be jealous of my son, to eat from his leftovers." Lucia arrogantly flipped her hair and kept her attention on the television, even though she knew Carl was glaring at her.

"How did you become so hateful?" Carl asked.

Lucia turned to look at Carl, with anger flashing in her eyes, "Whatever I am today, you made me so." Lucia walked out of his office.

Immediately she left her husband's office, she called the number of a business strategist someone had recommended. She planned to resurrect the Walton company after taking it off the Walton family. It would be her gift to her son, but first, she had to tell Damian all about the Walton family.

Chapter Fifteen

After Sandy was discharged from the hospital, Hector continued visiting her, until his father stepped in and forbade him from contacting Sandy.

"We do not want the family name dragged into her mess, especially since she was Damian's fiancée," Carl said.

He was not entirely wrong; the public blamed Sandy's suicidal instincts on Damian's betrayal. Hate mails had been sent to the manor, and even the company's social media handles were riddled with hate messages from those who sympathized with Sandy.

For three months Sandy battled with depression, with long periods of low state. There were times she could not find the will to leave her bed. The doctor diagnosed her with chronic depression and a lack of will to live. Her girlfriends did all they could to help, but there was no improvement. They decided to reach out to Damian to help. That day, Hailey went to Rem Energy to look for Damian.

"Mr. Remington is not in the country," the receptionist told her.

Disappointed and confused about how best to help her friend, Hailey turned to leave and ran into Hector.

"What are you doing here?" Hector asked. "How is Sandy?"

"She is not doing fine. The doctor diagnosed her with chronic depression. I am afraid one day she is going to slip into a coma. She is shutting down from lifer every day and we don't know how to help her." Hailey wiped a teardrop from her eye. "I came here to see Damian and ask that he talked to her, but it seems that bastard is on vacation."

"Damian is having problems of his own. It seems his marriage is on the rocks, especially with everything going on with Sandy," Hector said.

"It is so sad. We had hoped for them. There was no doubt they loved each other. Who would have thought that it would get to this point?" Hailey asked rhetorically.

"I am sorry about your friend," Hector said.

When Hector got to his office, he sat down and replayed everything Hailey said in his head. He had stayed away because of his stepbrother and their father. But he could not stay away anymore. In the few weeks he spent with Sandy, he came to like her, even though she was not in her best form. He believed when she said she was set up and knew nothing about Gold-leaf Energy being a dummy company.

"Are you going to allow the same man who abandoned you for years dictate how you live your life?" an inner voice asked him.

"No, I won't. I have come to see Sandy as my friend and now that she needs help, I will help her," Hector resolved in his heart.

Sandy lay in bed when Hector came. Hailey was surprised to see him, but she had noticed how much he cared for her friend.

"Sandy, someone is here to see you," Hailey said to Sandy.

"I don't want to see anyone. I have said that before."

"It's Hector. He is your friend, isn't he?"

"But he is also a Remington...nothing good can come out of there," Sandy replied.

"Hector took care of your hospital bills, you know, and he stayed by your side all the weeks you were suicidal. He does not deserve the way you are treating him," Hailey said beseechingly.

"He ran me over, so I don't need to thank him for taking care of the hospital bills. I can pay him if he wants!"

"How? You lay in bed all day. You are wasting your life away, without a job or any means of livelihood. So how do you expect to pay him?"

Sandy was vexed by what Hailey said and so she left her bed and stomped her way to the living room where Hector was sitting.

"What do you want? You want me to pay you for all you did. Hailey seems to think so!" Sandy yelled.

Hector was taken aback by her attitude, but he wondered if a sense of purpose was not what Sandy needed in her life. Working to pay him could be the purpose that would push her out of depression.

"Yes, I want you to pay me," Hector said.

Hailey was taken aback and looked at him with questioning eyes, but he maintained a straight face.

"But I don't want your money. I want you to work for me instead," Hector said.

Sandy became the manager of Hector's restaurant. She brought the knowledge she garnered working in Rem Energy and moved the restaurant to new heights. With Hector's help, she developed new recipes that brought in new types of customers. In under a month, Sandy remembered the tragedy of the past months with a dull pain. She did not think she was worthless but felt she could make something of her life. She was determined to prove to herself she had worth and every success she made with Hector's restaurant, became her success. Slowly, but surely, she was turning a new leaf. One day, Hector visited the restaurant and asked that they had lunch together.

"Then I think you should taste this new recipe I created myself," Sandy said with delight. She beckoned on the chief chef and asked him to serve them 'Hector Special.'

"You named it after me?" Hector was surprised.

"Aside from the fact that this is your restaurant, you were also the inspiration," Sandy replied.

Hector was happy about the change he noticed in Sandy. She laughed more and her color glowed. The only thing he did not agree with was her hair, which she now wore shorter.

"Why did you cut your hair?" Hector asked.

"It reminded me of my past," Sandy replied, with a small smile. "Damian loved my hair and never liked me tying it up. This is my way of saying 'fuck you.'"

"Wow." Hector burst into laughter. He felt happy that Sandy could talk about Damian, with a smile. He was happier than he was instrumental in her recovery.

"So, I came to give something to you," Hector said and brought out an envelope from his pocket, which he gave to Sandy.

Sandy opened the envelope and found a check to the tune of two hundred thousand dollars. "But why are you giving me this?"

"It is your salary for the months you have worked here. Did you think I was going to make you pay for me? I knew that was the only way to bring you out of the state you were in."

"Oh my God." Sandy stared at the check, with unbelieving eyes.

"Now, what are you going to do with it?" Hector asked.

"I am going to get an MBA degree," Sandy replied.

Hector nodded in approval. She was going to be all right after all.

Damian came down from the airplane at the private airstrip. It was only his mother who was there to receive him. Throughout his tour of Europe, she had kept in touch. His father became disappointed in him, after finding out that the Walton's were broke and so their relationship was strained. He was back in New York, determined to make a new beginning.

"Hello, mother." He kissed her both cheeks.

"My son, I am so glad you are back. It is time to take over the running of Rem Energy and force your father into retirement. It is the only way to make sure he never gives your right to his bastard son."

"Good idea, because I am giving Walton's back to their company. It is a step in fixing my marriage."

"While I wouldn't want that, it is your choice. Come on, it is time to go home."

Mother and son walked hand in hand to the waiting car.

True to his words, Damian gave back the company to the Walton's. The mansion his mother bought, was given to Nicole as a gift.

"Why?" Nicole was surprised.

"You lied to me, but at one point in time, I also did. I married you because I wanted to remain the Remington heir and that was not fair. I have reconciled myself with the things I have lost, and I am ready to make this marriage work," Damian replied.

Throughout the day, Nicole thought long and hard about her secret relationship with Colby. Damian had surprised her by wanting to make things work between them and it was only fair that she put in an effort.

"The first thing is to end my relationship with Colby," Nicole thought.

She could not stand looking at him in the eyes, so she called him on the phone and told him she wanted to work on her marriage. Colby took it hard, but since she refused to divorce Damian, he knew she was never his.

"I wish you good luck in all your heart seeks for," Colby said before hanging up.

That night, while Damian was out, Nicole decorated their room. She kept fresh flowers in glass jars and sprinkled some on the bed. She also bought scented candles and lit them around the bedroom. She came home early so she spent hours in the bathroom pampering herself. After this, she dons red lingerie and lets her blonde fall all over her face.

"Tonight, I am going to try and rekindle the passion we had the first time we dated," Nicole thought.

When Damian entered their bedroom, he was surprised at the atmosphere, but he understood when Nicole sashayed towards him.

"Do you think we can save this marriage? Let's find out if there is any passion left between us." Nicole undressed him and pushed him towards the bathroom. "Get cleaned up, baby."

When Damian came out of the bathroom, Nicole's red lingerie was lying on the bed, amid the flowers. Then he saw Nicole, all naked and oiled, with her fingers beckoning on him to come. With one finger, he unhooked the towel around his waist and let it fall to his feet. He took Nicole in his arms and trailed kisses down her naked body. As he ravished her, he tried to forget the woman whose body felt like home to him. He tried to forget Sandy, for he was trying to create a new beginning.

Chapter Sixteen

***

It has been three years since Sandy left Hector's employ. On this fateful day, she graduated with an MBA. The journey had been fierce, but everything she wanted to give up and fall back into depression, she remembered how much she wanted to prove to herself.

"Look at you, see how much you have become a strong woman," Hailey said to her as they stood in front of the Columbia Business School.

"You should raise your shoulders high. It is not a small feat to have an MBA degree," Bridget said.

"Congratulations my darling, you have come a long way and the only way from here is up." Spencer pulled her into her arms and kissed her hair.

"Be right back," Sandy said and rushed away. She was becoming emotional and did not want her friends to see the tears gathering fast in her eyes.

In the restroom, she stood before the mirror and took a long at herself. She had grown her hair back because she realized she loved her hair longer. Why would she cut her hair because she was angry at a man? Besides, she was no longer angry. She wished he had more backbone, but she could not blame him. In the three years, she had found religion and read her bible often. Because of the bible, she understood that human beings were like trees; they were never alone but had roots. Damian was rooted in his family and the luxury he had grown up in. She could not blame him if he could not let go of his roots for love.

"But I miss you, Damian. I wish you were here to see me today," Sandy said to the mirror. "Still, I know that perhaps I would have been certified with just being your wife and never finding my place in this world if you had not splintered my heart the way you did."

When Sandy realized she was crying, she wiped her eyes and smiled at her reflection. "Don't cry, Sandy. This is a new beginning."

Later that night, Sandy and her gang went to Lavo bar. It was as if they were coming back to the beginning, where it all happened. But this time, it was different; she was not the new girl who needed her friends to do a makeover before she could feel confident in her skin.

Sandy was a woman in her early thirties, self-assured and confident. She had added a bit of flesh and looked like the women she used to admire. Her black hair had a red tint at the top which gave her a sophisticated edge. For their celebratory night out, Sandy chose a midnight blue, sequined Balmain dress with a pair of Louboutin stilettos. One thing however was constant; Sandy did not drink alcohol.

She was nursing her cherry drink and enjoying her time with her friends, unaware that a man was checking her out. When Hailey and the girls went dancing with men they had picked up from the bar, a tall, average looking man, came to sit by her.

"Hi, beautiful." He smiled in a coquettish way, which made Sandy realize that what he lacked in looks, he made up for in-game.

"Hello, handsome." She flirted right back.

They made some talk, as he got her more of the cherry drink. She was comfortable with him, but there were no fireworks. She found herself comparing their meeting with when she met Damian. There was no chemistry, but she liked him.

He called himself Alan and he had nice eyes that smiled even when he was not smiling.

"I like you already, Sandy. You are my kind of woman," Alan said. "Let's have coffee tomorrow."

"It would be my pleasure." Sandy smiled at him.

After Alan left, her friends came back. They had seen the man with her and giggled their approval.

"He looks cool, Sandy," Bridget said.

"I have watched you turn down every man who came too close, except this one," Hailey stated.

"I think I am ready." Sandy giggled. She felt it that she was finally ready to move on.

"We should make a toast," Spencer said, and the girls grabbed their glasses.

"To new beginnings," Hailey said.

"Yes," they all chorused and clinked their glasses.

Three years had also taken a toll on Damian in a good way. He was now a father of two lovely boys, Scott and Preston. He and Nicole were closer than ever, and they led a happy life. His mother was still her aristocratic self, with more power, since Carl was removed as CEO. Her son deferred to her in all things. With Damian's prodding, she was friendlier with Hector, especially when he was no longer a threat to her son. Carl had gotten over his resentment of his son, because of the takeover. He enjoyed life making other investments and having any woman he wanted. Life was beautiful with the Remington's, but sometimes it becomes so sunny when it is about to rain.

One morning, Nicole hurried her boys into the car, so she could drive them to her parents. It was the weekend and she wanted to enjoy it with her husband, without having to cater to the children.

"You know you don't have to send them away. I am here to take care of them," Lucia said standing by the front door.

"Mother, with all the engagements you have this weekend, I am not sure you can cope with two super active boys," Nicole replied and they both laughed.

As she made to enter her car, she felt a sharp pain in her right ribs. She buckled over and held on to the door of her car for support.

"Nicole, what is wrong?" Lucia came over to her.

"I felt pain in my ribs, but it is gone now," Nicole said and managed a smile.

"If you say so."

On the drive to her parents, Nicole kept wondering what the cause of the sharp pain was because it had been occurring throughout the week.

"I will go see the doctor after we are back from our weekend trip," Nicole thought to herself.

However, she could not let go of the fear that it could be something bad. She feared anything that would destroy the happiness she had built in her life.

"Oh God..." she heaved a breath and returned her focus to the road.

While Nicole was enjoying a weekend vacation with her husband in Las Vegas, Sandy went with Alan to Newark, for his cousin's wedding. It was a weekend of partying and solemn wedding ceremonies. Sandy felt comfortable with Alan's family and he noticed.

"Alan has never brought a girl home. You must be special," Alan's mother told Sandy, who only smiled in response.

After the wedding, that Sunday night, Alan took her around the city of Newark. They ate in restaurants he usually ate in when he was younger and went to all his favorite places in the city. On their drive back home, Alan suddenly stopped the car.

"Sandy, I have a question to ask and you only get to answer this once. After today, I will never ask you again," Alan said.

"Ask me." Sandy's voice was uncertain, but she smiled.

Alan brought out a ring from his pocket and said, "Will you marry me?"

"What?" Sandy gasped.

"You can only answer yes or no," Alan replied.

Sandy looked into his eyes; it was too sudden, but this year she had done many things on impulse and they had turned outright. She enjoyed all her time with Alan, but was that enough to marry him, she wondered.

"Yes, or no." Alan looked at her intently.

"Yes," Sandy said.

"Thank you for saying yes." Alan slipped the ring on to her finger and embraced her.

This was the second time a man was putting a ring on her finger and she could not help but compare. Damian was a trust fund child, heir to a wealthy family, while Alan was a simple, middle-class family. Damian was a businessman, in charge of a large conglomerate, Alan was a doctor who did not know much than cutting up people, to make them well. She looked down at the simple cut diamond ring and smiled. Damian had engaged her with the most expensive ring at the time, but Alan, like the simple man he was, had opted for something simple.

"I am going to be happy, at all cost," Sandy told herself.

After a fun-filled weekend at Las Vegas, during which the pain became more frequent and lasted longer, Nicole came back to New York with her husband. They stopped over at her parents' house to get the boys and take them to school. After dropping the boys at school, they drove to the manor.

When Nicole tried to alight from the car, the pain came again, this time sharper than before, so much that she yelped.

"Nicole!" Damian was out of the car in the blink of an eye and went over to her.

"It is so painful," Nicole cried.

"What is?" Damian asked.

"The pain in my ribs and now my chest." Nicole winched and moaned in pain.

Damian rushed to the front door and banged on it. When the butler opened, he ordered him to call the family doctor. Then he carried Nicole in his arms into the house.

The doctor came and by this time Nicole was crying sorely from the pain. The doctor took one look at her and told them to bring her to the hospital, where tests could be run on her.

"What is wrong with her, doctor?" Damian's voice was filled with worry.

"It is too early to say," the doctor replied.

Nicole was driven to the hospital where she was admitted immediately, with different tests being run on her. After an hour, the doctor called Damian into his office.

"It is bad," the doctor began.

"What is?" Damian asked.

"Your wife's health is deteriorating. She has lung cancer," the doctor said.

"What!" Damian got up from the chair like he had been stung.

"I am sorry, Mr. Remington. She has just three months to live. Lung cancer is the most fatal form of cancer because it does not show any symptoms until it is too late."

"Doctor, what are you trying to tell me? Are you saying I will lose my wife?"

"I am sorry, sir."

"No, don't be sorry. Give me a solution. I want her to undergo chemotherapy," Damian said.

"Chemotherapy will not work at this stage. It is too progressed at this point."

Damian banged on the doctor's table, "Don't tell me what to do. I want her to have chemo."

When Nicole was told of her condition, she asked the doctor, "How long do I have?"

The doctor could not reply, because he was touched by the pain on Nicole's face.

"I have three months to live and you want me to spend it having chemotherapy? I will lose my beautiful hair and spend less time with my loved ones, fighting a disease that has already won?" Nicole asked, looking up to her grief-stricken husband.

"I won't have chemotherapy..." Nicole said, but Damian cut her off.

"What are you saying? You cannot give up like that. There is still a chance of survival."

"What are the chances of survival, doctor?" Nicole asked.

"Six percent, ma'am," the doctor replied in a low voice.

Nicole held back sobs and managed to say, "I will spend the remaining months of my life, being happy and being loved."

The next three months were a struggle; Damian watched his wife die slowly. She lost all her healthy weight and became thin. By the last month, she had become bedridden and was mostly unconscious. Whenever she was conscious, she wrote what she wanted to say on paper. Her sons, Scott and Preston were stopped from seeing her, as they were taken to live with the Walton's. Damian made Hector the acting CEO, so he could spend time with his dying wife. This was against his mother's better judgment, so she kept a strict eye on Hector's dealings.

One fateful night, Damian had fallen asleep on the couch beside Nicole's bed, and suddenly he heard his name in a clear voice. He opened his eyes and Nicole beckoned to him.

"Come closer," she said in a hoarse voice.

"You can speak again. Are you..."

"No Damian, I am not. I have a few important things to say."

"Until my dying day, I held the love of another man in my heart. His name is Colby and he was my great love," Nicole said. A tear trickled down the side of her face as she spoke.

"After you gave back the company to my parents, I was ready to make our marriage work, at the expense of my great love. So, I want you to send it to him. Check my phone for Colby and tell him to come. I want to behold his face one last time."

Damian started to go, but Nicole held his hand. For such a frail woman, her grip was firm. "Give me water."

Damian always kept a bottle of water by her bedside, so he poured a glass for her. He could not cry, but his heart was bleeding. He felt unfortunate because it seemed happiness always came but left just as quickly as it came. First, he had loved Sandy, and then they had been torn apart, and then he had built happiness with Nicole, but even she was leaving.

"I never let go of the love I have for Colby, and that is why I know you still love Sandy. So many waters under the bridge, but the flower of love remains by the bank. Look for her and this time, never let her go," Nicole said, and then she closed her eyes.

"Nicole! Don't leave me," Damian screamed.

"I am still here...howbeit for a short while." Nicole smiled weakly and closed her eyes again. "I want to rest."

Every time Damian went close to her nose to see if she was still breathing and every time, he listened to her slow, labored breathing. So, he told himself she would stay one more day. Oh, how wrong he was.

Throughout the night, Damian did not check for Nicole's breathing, because he fell into a deep sleep and had a dream. In the dream, he saw Sandy and she was happy. She was alone, but she was smiling and looking at someone he could not see. When he woke up from the dream, he could see the first light of dawn. He got up from the couch and went to Nicole. He took her hand and was startled by its coldness. When he bent to check for her breathing, he found none.

"Nicole! Nicole!" Damian cried with a loud voice that woke up the occupants of the manor.

Everyone rushed to their bedroom and saw Damian shaking Nicole and begging her not to leave him.

"My son," Lucia said and wiped a teardrop from her eye. She went over to her son and pried him away from his dead wife. "Don't just stand there, call 911," she turned to the house staff and said.

Chapter Seventeen

O ne year had passed after Nicole's death. Damian had stayed off women, focused only on Rem Energy and his boys. He had looked for Sandy, surprised to find that she had been in New York all along. Sadly, she was married to a doctor, and she was happy. He remembered the dream he had on the night Nicole died and realized it was what the dream was trying to tell him. She was happy, and he should let her be, despite Nicole's words.

Sandy was indeed happy, happier she had thought possible. "Truly, love isn't all there is to marriage," she told her friends.

"Especially the fiery love you and Damian shared," Hailey replied.

It was only Hailey and Sandy now; Bridget had relocated to Europe after her wedding to a prince from a small country in Europe. Spencer had also moved to Canada because her company sent her to head a new branch. Hailey had stayed unmarried, not due to lack of marriage proposals, but she had become closer to Sandy.

"Who is Damian?" they heard someone ask. They turned and saw Alan with two glasses of juice.

"Are you eavesdropping now?" Hailey teased.

"No, I just overheard," Alan replied with a smile.

"He was my ex," Sandy said looking down.

"He was her billionaire, great love," Hailey quipped.

"Interesting. What happened?" Alan asked.

"The past stays in the past, that's our rule." Sandy took a glass of juice from him.

"All right then, I will be in my study." Alan kissed the top of her hair. "Your hair is all over the place, get a haircut, will you?" Alan added before leaving.

In his study, Alan did not pore over the patient's report or worked on his research. He went to the internet and typed in 'Billionaire Damian.' He waited for a few seconds before the results rolled out. Only one name stood out; Damian Remington. He read everything he could find on him and then he read about the love story between him and Sandy. When he read that his wife passed away a year ago, he became thoughtful.

"Could this be the hand of fate?" he thought to himself.

Damian had barely sat down in his office when his secretary rushed in. He looked up from the reports from the departments and asked her what she wanted.

"A man is demanding to see you. He said he is from Sandy," the willowy secretary said.

"Sandy?" he got up from his seat abruptly. "Send him in."

Damian watched the man walk towards him and wondered who he was. He could not help but remember that dream again.

"Who are you and how can I help you?" Damian asked the moment he showed the man to a seat.

"You can call me Alan. I am Sandy's husband. I need your help, for Sandy's sake."

Damian stood up immediately, "Don't tell me she is sick too."

"She is not, I am," Alan said.

"Can I get you something to drink?" Damian asked as he accessed the man Sandy married.

"I am fine," Alan replied, smiling with his eyes. "I came here because my wife was talking with her friend and your name came up. I read about your love story on the net and I know that kind of love does not die. I came here because I also found out that your wife is dead. I am sorry for your loss."

"Thank you."

"I found out I was sick with Leukemia and had only a year to live. I thought I would die alone, but then I met Sandy. I never told her of my death sentence, because I wanted to be happy for the last moments of my life. I have lived longer than the doctors gave me, but I know death will come any time now."

Damian was forced to remember the last three months of Nicole's life and it made his heartbreak that Sandy would be put through the same agony.

"I am so sorry," Damian said.

"Don't be," Alan replied. "I want you to be there for Sandy when I go. She never stopped loving you for a day. Even when I never knew about you, I always knew there was someone who held her heart, because she never quite gave it to me."

Damian nodded his head because he understood. He never quite gave his heart to Nicole, even though he was happy with her.

"Promise me you would never leave her." Alan took Damian's hand and held it without letting it go.

"I promise," Damian said.

Alan stretched his hand and gave Damian Sandy's contact card. "See you around. Now, I can die knowing that my Sandy is never alone."

"Sweetheart, I am off for my business meeting. They just sent a car to bring me," Sandy said. Then she kissed her husband on the cheek, before walking away.

But then, she stopped and turned to look at him, "Is it just me or are you losing weight?"

"I have been under a lot of pressure, Sandy. Go and break a leg, when you come back, we will talk," Alan replied with a bright smile.

"All right see you later." Sandy walked out the door, not knowing that it was the last time she would see her husband smile.

Chapter Eighteen

———⟡———

The car drove down a familiar street and it made Sandy feel nostalgic. She could not put her finger on the reason she felt this way until the car stopped in front of the manor.

"What is going on here?" Sandy asked.

"You are going to meet your client," the driver replied and drove the car inside as soon as the gate opened.

Sandy alighted from the car slowly, as the memories came flooding back. She looked on just as Lucia came out the door. She was taken aback when she saw Sandy.

"You...I almost did not recognize you," Lucia said.

"Good day, ma'am." Sandy gave an uneasy smile.

"Hmmn..." Lucia smiled tightly and walked away.

Sandy was led into the house where Hector was waiting for her. "Hi, my best woman in the world."

"What, you are the client?" Sandy asked in surprise.

"Sure...is that how you greet a friend you have not seen in years though?" Hector said and opened his hand wide.

Sandy went to him and embraced him. "How have you been?"

"I have been well, and I am expanding my restaurant in Europe. I need you to..."

"I am married now and cannot just up and leave for Europe. But I can help you manage everything from here."

"I have a manager, so rest easy. I need a business strategist, because it is a new terrain, and this is where you come in."

"Sandy?" she heard the voice and knew immediately who it was. She turned and stared right at Damian. She could not take her eyes as she noticed the subtle changes in him. She looked at his finger and was surprised to find that there was no ring there. Did he divorce Nicole, she wondered?

"Hi," Sandy said with an uneasy smile.

"Dad, Louis just called. We are having a sleepover," Scott said, on his father's trail.

"I am not going," Preston quipped.

"Are these your kids?" Sandy asked, too late to hold in her thoughts.

"Yes, they are. It has been a long time. Can we sit down and have a shot sometime?" Damian asked, while his eyes begged her not to say no.

"All right," Sandy replied.

"I am proud of who you have become, Sandy," Damian said before walking away.

"Uncle Hector..."

"Not now, Scott. Your uncle is busy with business." Damian called his sons to come with him.

"All right." Scott rolled his eyes and went with his father and Preston.

"They are adorable," Sandy said, with a voice laden with emotion.

"Do you have kids? You never kept in touch."

"No, I don't."

They sat down and discussed Sandy's business until it was late into the night.

"You should have dinner with us. I think Damian would appreciate it."

"I don't think so..." Sandy started to say.

"Nicole passed away...cancer." Hector looked at her pointedly.

"Oh my God!" Sandy gasped. Tears came to her eyes because she imagined what pain Damian would have gone through. No wonder he did not wear a ring, she thought.

"Excuse me, sir Hector. Ma'am Lucia says dinnertime is in ten minutes," one of the house staff said.

"All right, thank you," Hector said and then turned to Sandy. "Have dinner with us."

"All right," Sandy agreed.

Dinner was a quiet affair. Seeing Sandy again brought back memories for everyone except the children. Carl Remington was absent because he was away on a hunting trip, no doubt with a woman on his arm. For Lucia, it made her remember Nicole and all they did together to keep Damian and Sandy apart. She did not regret it. For Damian, he wished he stayed and fought for their love. He soon found out that Sandy never had a relationship with Mitch; Nicole confessed that it was all her plan when they were starting afresh. He forgave her, but he blamed himself for falling for it. Knowing what he knew about her husband, he wanted to pull her into his arms and tell her everything would be all right.

The silence was broken by the chirping of Sandy's phone. She excused herself from the table and went into the hallway to receive the call.

"Hello, Sandy here," she said into the phone.

"You need to come to the hospital right now because your husband is dying," the caller said. "City hospital."

"What!" Sandy exclaimed.

In a flash, Damian was out of his chair and ran to Sandy. "Are you, all right?"

"My husband is in the hospital, he is dying they say," Sandy went back to the table, grabbed her bag, and began to walk away.

Damian grabbed her and wrapped his arms around her. "I understand, I am here."

She relaxed into the hug and it felt like home. But when she was tempted to stay forever, Sandy pushed him away, "You don't understand anything! Whenever I am happy, something comes and snatches my happiness away. It happened to you...I can't lose Alan too."

"Sandy..." Damian tried to reach for her.

"No, Damian. No." Sandy left the house, without looking back, but Hector ran after her and offered to drive her to the hospital.

Sandy stood before the mirror and looked at herself. She had been through a lot in the past days. Her house was filled with Alan's grieving family members. They had all known, except her. Would she have rejected to marry him, if she knew, she wondered to herself?

"I would have been better prepared. The rug was just pulled from under me, while I was still dancing," she thought.

That night when she left the Remington Manor, she went to the hospital and was taken immediately to the ICU where her husband was fighting for his life. When she saw him on the bed, it appears he had aged ten years since the last time she saw him. She looked up to drive the tears back because she had vowed not to cry. She wanted to show him she was strong, so he would find the strength to stay.

"I stayed longer because of you. You gave me more time, with your devotion and care," Alan said the moment he saw her.

"If I was so devoted, why didn't I notice you were sick? How did I just find out you have cancer?"

"I hid it well. The safe which I told you held my documents, were filled with drugs and I made sure you never saw them. The drugs helped mask my symptoms," Alan replied.

"But why did you hide it from me?" Sandy took his hand and held on strongly, as though she wanted to stop him from leaving her.

"I saw how happy you were with me and I did not want to taint your happiness. If I did, it would have killed me faster. I am sorry I was selfish."

Sandy could not bring herself to cry; she just laid on his chest and together they slept off. She was woken up by a shrill cry; it was Alan's mother. She came in and saw Alan was no longer breathing and even then, Sandy did not cry. She was too shocked to cry.

Even now, she stood before the mirror stoically, without a tear to shed. She was sad, her heart was breaking, but the tears could not come. All around her, people planned Alan's funeral, but she felt detached from it all. It was as if her heart was waiting for someone before it could beat again.

"Ma'am, there is someone there to see you," her housekeeper said. She was an elderly woman with gray hair and kind eyes. She looked on Sandy with sympathy and so much sadness, that Sandy was forced to smile, just to reassure her she was all right.

Sandy followed the housekeeper to the living room, where she saw Hector and Damian. Hector started to come to her, but he stopped when he saw her eyes were on Damian instead.

"Damian," she whispered, and then she ran to him. He wrapped her in his arms and then the floodgate was thrown wide open because Sandy cried her eyes out.

"Alan is gone, my husband is gone!" Sandy cried, surprising everyone.

"Fate is cruel...it hates me being happy," Sandy wailed.

"Don't talk that way, my child. The Lord gives, and he takes away," Alan's mother said. There were tears in her eyes even as she talked. Her eyes were swollen from crying already, for Alan was her only child.

"She is right, ma'am," the housekeeper added. "One day, you will find happiness and maybe it is already here."

"It is going to be all right," Damian said and kissed her hair, even as he wrapped his arms tight around her. He wanted to take her pain away, but he did not know-how. He remembered his promise to Alan and he knew that everything had happened to them both, for a reason.

"I am here now and this time, I will never leave you." Damian looked into her eyes as he said this.

Epilogue

———◇———

Lucia stood at one of her favorite spots in the Remington manor and watched Scott and Preston below on their bikes.

"My grandchildren," she thought.

Speaking of grandchildren, there would soon be an addition to her grandchildren. Sandy was pregnant with Damian's child, just barely a year after losing her husband. She did not know what she felt about Sandy, but she knew she was happy about another grandchild.

Even before Nicole died, her boys had become so close to their grandmother, that when they woke in the morning, they ran into her room to kiss her, before talking to anybody in the house. They loved her, and she loved them right back, which showed in the way she bought properties in their name.

"I wish Sandy would give me a granddaughter this time. Oh, how I wish for a princess to spoil rotten," Lucia thought as a smile stole on her face.

"It must be nice thoughts you are having, seeing such a lovely smile," someone said behind her.

Lucia turned from where she was standing at the East balcony, to see a heavily pregnant Sandy. She turned back to continue looking at her grandsons, without saying a word. However, that did not stop Sandy from coming close to stand by her.

"You know, I love your son and I think we were made for each other. But if you say the world, I will give birth to this child and leave his life forever," Sandy said.

"You would do that?" Lucia turned to look at her, with a quizzical look in her eyes.

"Why do you think I have not agreed to marry Damian? It is not because of my late husband's family, but because of you. I cannot enter your family unless you permit me."

"Are you not already one of us? You are carrying a Remington in your womb and you have been living here," Lucia replied.

"I have been living here because..."

"Because you think you cannot do without him," Lucia interjected. "Sandy, even when I did not like you, I still respected you. You were the kind of woman I would have wanted my daughter to become if I had one. After what Damian did to you, you just forgave him!"

Sandy was taken aback at the direction the conversation had taken.

When she came here to look for Lucia, it was to try and find out why the woman did not want her, even after many years and with so many heartaches. She did not expect that they would be discussing her choices. However, she was quick to know the source of Lucia's words. Since living in the Remington manor, she had noticed the deteriorating relationship between the patron and matron of the Remington family.

"If you love someone, you would forgive them," Sandy said.

"Some sins cannot be forgiven. Besides, it has never been love between me and Carl. We married for the sake of our families, just as Nicole and Damian did." Lucia turned to look at Sandy again. "Damian always loved you, but he had a good marriage with Nicole. They settled their differences and created a haven for their kids. Nicole was lucky."

"Why didn't you leave?" Sandy asked.

"It's funny, but I can't."

"You can do anything you want. Nothing has stopped you before," Sandy said. She did not mean it that way, but she could not help that it sounded like she was referring to the things Lucia did to keep her away from Damian. When the silence became awkward, Sandy turned to leave.

"I have never quite apologized for what I did before..." Lucia started, and it made Sandy stop.

"I was not referring to that, I promise," Sandy interjected.

"Even so, you deserve an apology. I did what I thought was best for my family. It is what I have always done since I was a child. Family always came first," Lucia continued.

"It is also the reason you never left," Sandy said, with a new understanding of the woman standing before her.

"You are smart and for some reason, I am happy you are here, right now, with this family," Lucia said and this time, she was the one who turned to leave.

Sandy knew she would not get any other validation of her relationship with Damian, other than what Lucia just said. A smile broke on her face, the same time a pain ripped through her.

"Oh my God!" The scream tore through her lips.

Lucia had not gone far, so she turned and rushed to Sandy, who was holding on to her abdomen.

"What is wrong?" Lucia asked.

"I think the baby is coming," Sandy said in between raspy breaths.

"Oh my, anybody there. Damian!" Lucia called out.

Two house staff ran out and when they saw Sandy writhing in pain, they rushed back in to call the driver.

When Sandy opened her eyes, the Remington family was gathered around her, including Carl Remington.

"She is awake!" Lucia exclaimed.

"Where is my baby? I want to see my baby," Sandy said.

"Nurse, where is the baby?" Lucia asked. She sounded so chirpy and happy.

She had never left Sandy's side since they brought her to the hospital, not even when Damian came to join them at the hospital. Throughout Sandy's labor ward experience, Lucia stayed by her side just as a mother would.

"Coming through..." Damian said as he was led in, holding the baby.

There were appreciative sounds as the baby was put in Sandy's arms. The pink baby was asleep, but she still managed to hold everyone's attention.

"Oh my, it is a little princess...my very own princess," Sandy cooed.

"I asked God for a granddaughter and he gave me." Lucia adjusted the blanket over the baby's little pink fingers.

"Sandy, I never wanted our princess to be born without you having my name. Now that she is here, will you marry me?" Damian asked kneeling.

Sandy looked to Lucia, who nodded her head in approval. "Yes!"

"Good! Get the priest, he is just outside," Damian said.

"You brought a priest?" Sandy was surprised.

The priest was called in and right there in the presence of the Remington clan, Sandy and Damian exchanged their marital vows.

"I love you, Sandy."

"I love you, Damian."

"Where is my new sister?" Everyone heard a little voice say.

Scott and Preston pushed through everyone, so they could come close to the bed.

"Aww, she is so little," Scott said.

"Yes, and she needs her big brothers to protect her at all times," Sandy said.

"I will protect her. See my arms," Preston said, pumping his arms.

"Me too," Scott added.

Sandy pulled the two boys to herself and kissed their foreheads. Damian could not bear the sight of his family; he burst into tears.

"I do not know what I did to deserve a second chance at being with the one I love, but I will never take it for granted, dear wife."

"Hmmn, wife. I like the sound of that." Sandy kissed her new husband. In her heart, she missed her family and she knew her joy would never be complete without them.

"How soon can we go to Oklahoma?" she whispered into Damian's ears.

"As soon as you can fly, wife," Damian replied.

THE END.